COUPLINGS

COUPLINGS

A Book of Stories by
RICHARD HALL

Grey Fox Press
San Francisco

Copyright © 1981, 1980, 1979, 1977, 1976 by Richard W. Hall

Grateful acknowledgment is made to the editors of the following magazines where some of these stories were first published: *Christopher Street, Gay News* (London), *GPU News, Gaysweek/Arts and Letters, Paragraph: A Quarterly of Gay Fiction* and *Vector*. "A Touch of Fat" was first published in *A True Likeness: Lesbian and Gay Writing Today* (1980), and is reprinted by permission of Sea Horse Press Limited.

The cover drawing by Doug Krohn is altered from the original, first printed by Eldon E. Murray in *GPU News*, and is used here with his permission and that of the artist.

Second printing, 1982.

Library of Congress Cataloging in Publication Data

Hall, Richard Walter
   Couplings : a book of stories.

   1. Homosexuality—fiction. 1. Title.
PS3558.A3735C68   813'.54   80-26609
ISBN 0-912516-58-5 (pbk.)

Distributed by The Subterranean Company,
P.O. Box 10233, Eugene, Oregon 97440.

for Arthur
a friend for all seasons

Contents

Preface	ix
The Prisoner of Love	1
The Taste of Spring	12
Colors	26
Death in San Juan	57
The Servant Problem	76
The Household God	90
The Judgment of Midas	98
The Koan	113
The Bad Penny	126
A Touch of Fat	152
The Boy Who Would Be Real	168

Preface

THE SHORT STORY has fallen on hard times, due partly to economics and partly to changed reader habits. The popular magazines like *Collier's* and *Liberty* that once nourished it have foundered, taking with them the incentive for writers to master the art of the miniature. Other magazines still with us, like *Harper's* and *The Atlantic,* now restrict their fiction to one entry per issue. Publishers tell us that short story collections, especially the omnibus anthology by many authors, don't sell well. It seems that readers don't like the rapid shift of setting, character and mood that short story collections entail; they prefer to settle in for a long read with one book—in other words, a binge. The shorter spans of their attention are reserved for newspapers and television.

This poses problems for writers fond of the short story because its strengths match their own. They must either train themselves out of their fondness and learn to handle the novel, or resign themselves to limited opportunities. Under this kind of pressure, even masters like John Cheever and Katherine Anne Porter have forced their writing into longer, uncongenial forms and produced work that is not their best.

It is with a certain degree of pessimism, then, that I launch this collection of my own stories, knowing all too well that a novel would command more of everything—reviewer attention, reader interest, publicity and sales. I find I have no choice in the matter. My imagination thrives on the exigencies of the brief form; my notebooks are full of people, scenes and themes that fit only into short stories.

The major attraction for me, I suppose, is the necessity for tightness and economy. Every effect must be calculated; every sentence must pay off. Short stories, as Jane Austen described her work in a letter to her brother, require the use of a fine brush on a little bit of ivory. The precision and difficulty of such effort appeals to me in a way that the novel, with its roomy spaces, its opportunity for digression, its carelessly cumulative effects, does not.

However, my obsession would probably not have produced stories, given the bad economics of it all, were it not for the emergence in recent years of a new publishing phenomenon—the gay magazine. Most of these stories first appeared in such publications as *GPU News, Paragraph, Vector, Christopher Street, Gaysweek* and *Gay News* of London. The existence of these media and the readiness of their editors to publish serious writing has given us a mini-Renaissance in the gay short story. A new genre, or subgenre, is in the making, proving once again that C. Northcote Parkinson omitted an important law from his canon—"The amount of good writing on any subject will expand to fill the number of blank press pages available." Gay publications, filling a historical vacuum, have done for stories by gay writers what the *Evening Chronicle* did for Dickens and *Harper's* did for Henry James—shaped our imagination, imposed a form and found us an audience. Thus, a dying literary genre has been given a new life—a fact confirmed by the recent appearance of a half-dozen anthologies of stories culled from the gay press.

Another equally compelling reason for the vitality of the gay short story is that now, for the first time, direct fictional expression of our sexuality is permitted. Until recently, the higher gay erotics could not be specified, the details of gay dalliance could not be dramatized. In the past, this has given us a huge literature of indirection—stories like "The Pupil," "Paul's Case," "Hands," "The Story of a Panic." One would think such euphemism and discretion would have disappeared by now, but editors of general magazines still shy away from explicitness, still insist that the door to the gay bedroom remain closed, believing that "our truth" cannot be "their truth." Only in our own magazines can we be free.

One result of this is that the sexual encounter is often at the core of our fiction. Gay writers, militant in this as in other matters, will no longer tolerate indirection. They reject discreet, allusive stories about the repressed celibate, the tomboy, the sensitive young man, the fighter for women's rights. Although they may start with such characters, they will end up in new, flamboyant places—the night-town of the gay world, its streets, bars, rallies, zaps and discos. And if these locales do not interest the writer, then gay domestic life—the marriage bed itself—may be explored without hypocrisy or false shame.

Which brings me to my own stories. It was only after assembling them for publication that I realized how related they were in theme and how naturally they fell under the title *Couplings*. Because couples and coupling, in both a passionate and a spiritual sense, are their text. Doubleness is central to my vision. At the root of each story is a pair, male or female, struggling with, for or against their bond. I am concerned with the suffering that arrives on our doorstep in the shape of a friend, a lover, an ex-lover. For this I will undoubtedly be called a romantic. It is a label I acknowledge, hoping that the ironies and defeats which my characters endure will keep critics from calling me sentimental too.

A word about some of the individual stories. One of them, "The Prisoner of Love," which first appeared as a story in the San Francisco magazine *Vector,* may be more familiar as a play of the same name expanded from the story. It was first performed at The Glines in New York in 1978, directed by Peter Dowling, and revived for a summer run in 1979 at the Spike Bar, also in New York.

Three of the stories, "Death in San Juan," "The Taste of Spring," and "Colors," are the remnants of a very ambitious plan of a few years ago. My idea was to do a switch on various literary masterworks, using their plot or theme as the basis for stories which would undo some evasion or injustice in the original. I planned to call this series "Tales from Literature." That I got no farther than three stories is proof either of my inadequacy or common sense or both. The careful reader probably needs no clue in order to decipher the disguises of the stories, but might be interested in my motives for writing them.

"Death in San Juan" was spun off from *Death in Venice,* which has long irritated me because of the way Thomas Mann equates Aschenbach's love for Tadzio with plague and death. What, I wondered, would happen if a gay man's love for a heterosexual family brought him into contact with the same fatal force? By matching heterosexuality, not homosexuality, with destruction, wouldn't I right the imbalance of the Mann story?

Another masterpiece that has always disturbed me is Joseph Conrad's *Heart of Darkness.* Anyone who has been forced, as I have, to teach this story to a college literature class composed of both black and white students, knows how painful the experience can be. Black students, quite justifiably, resent Conrad's colonial parallel between a dark skin and moral evil. The story's assumptions, language and characterization are violently racist. It was to right this wrong, to reverse the racist myth, that I wrote "Colors"—hoping to show that barbarism may erupt among people of any skin pigmentation.

The third tale from literature is "The Taste of Spring," derived from *The Aspern Papers* by Henry James. I have always wondered what those famous papers actually consisted of—what revelations of love and lust, unspecified by the author, were contained in them. Using one of our own legends, the lesbians of Paris between the wars, I constructed a new version of the Jamesian drama, still moldily rococo, but naming the actual contents of Miss Bordereau's dusty trunk.

I like to think that none of these stories is as simple as I have described it and that, like the other stories in the book, each arises from needs deeper than mere ideology. Whether my readers will agree with such an estimate remains to be seen.

RICHARD HALL

New York, January 1981

COUPLINGS

The Prisoner of Love

THE SOLUTION came to me in mid-February as I was sitting on the beach in Puerto Rico, propelled there by a natural laziness and a small income that permitted me to indulge it. Looking at the sea—green jello with meringue topping—it occurred to me that Puerto Rico might be the perfect gift for Martin Chrisman. Why not invite him down, all expenses paid, for a week? I turned to the seawall and checked out the beach boys lounging there. They were looking at the sunbathers hungrily. No doubt about it. Puerto Rico was just the thing for Martin—Martin who had done so much for all of us.

The Movement! Martin lived, breathed, defecated the Movement. Gay oppression, gay pride, gay history, gay love—these brought tears to his eyes, eloquence to his speech. At every march, every zap, Martin was in the front rank, hung with buttons, his fists pumping as he gave the yells. Between times he lived quietly, devoting his time to writing and publishing such pamphlets as *The Warrior Apprentice in Classical Greece*, *Homophile Themes in Provençal Poetry*, *Ernst Rohm and the Secret Pact with Hitler*.

Yes, Martin, who lived in poverty for the sake of his principles, needed to be repaid.

I called New York that night. Martin's voice was high and fluty, but underneath I could hear the stubbornness—the very same that had produced *Homoeroticism and the Anarchist Movement, 1848–1914*.

"It's Jackson. I'm in Puerto Rico."

"Oh, Jackson. What is it?"

"I want you come down here where it's warm."

"I'm busy now."

"Just for a week. As my guest."

A pause at the other end. "Well, I've never been to Puerto Rico. You know we stole it from Spain."

"So I heard. I'll send you the ticket in the morning."

Another pause. "Do you have a typewriter? I'm doing a paper on the berdaches and the Sioux."

"Martin—this is play, not work."

"This is extremely important..." But he didn't get any further because the Puerto Rico Telephone Company, in its infinite wisdom, chose to cut us off.

The plane disgorged two hundred passengers before Martin emerged, carrying a straw suitcase. He seemed out of place among those gaudy vacationers—a young-old person with an air of solitude that enveloped him like a caul. He blinked when he saw me and put out a thin hairless paw. I felt momentarily uneasy. I had never been alone with him for a long stretch of time. Perhaps my discomfort communicated itself, because he answered in monosyllables as we drove home, and made no comment at all on the spectacular views.

At the apartment, which was right on the beach, he put down his suitcase and stood in the center of the room. I walked to the terrace doors and threw them back. "Take a look!" I sang out.

He moved forward reluctantly, as if it were a punishment of some kind. On the terrace he removed his glasses—they were hornrims—and squinted against the light.

"How do you like it?" I asked finally.

He looked displeased. It was clear that the Atlantic Ocean had failed him in some way. Then he peered downward. "Who are all those boys?"

"Oh, locals." I paused. "Hoping to make out with a tourist."

He put his glasses back on. "You mean they're hustling?" His voice was full of outrage.

"Well—yeah." I felt suddenly apologetic.

"They've been forced into prostitution by American imperialist policies," he announced.

Several replies took shape in my mind—defensive, explanatory, aggressive. But I managed to repress them all. We had a long week ahead of us. The best time to avoid an argument is before it starts.

I gave him a cold avocado salad for lunch. While he ate, he told me that a Chinese restaurant in his neighborhood had been caught with a freezer full of dead cats. When I gagged at the news, a bitter pleat formed on his lips—the first expression of pleasure since his arrival.

After lunch we went down to the beach. A shower had just ended and the sky was printed with a rainbow. Martin eyed the arc suspiciously, as if it were a temptation that had to be resisted.

The beach boys had taken refuge under an awning. I knew one of them—Armando—but I didn't wave. He'd soon be over for a cigarette. Martin took out dark glasses and clipped them over his spectacles. The two layers of glass made him look as if he were undergoing an eye examination. He lay back on the blanket, his thin chest gleaming whitely.

Armando spotted us eventually and strolled over, grinning. "You better cover up," he said to Martin, hunkering down, "you gonna fry." He put out a hand to me. "Gotta cigarette?"

I gave him one, watching him cup the match against the trade wind. His face was khaki-colored, with heavy eyebrows. He was wearing jeans and a shirt printed with the signs of the zodiac. It was unbuttoned to his navel. The silky black chest hairs made a cruciform. As Martin applied oil to his shoulders, he sneaked glances at Armando.

"Are you an *independente*?" he asked at last.

"*Independentista*?" Armando shook his head. "Not me, man. The day the Puerto Ricans take over, I'm getting out."

Martin trained his double glasses on him. "You're in favor of the colonial oppression of Puerto Rico?"

Armando gave him a disgusted look. "You believe that propaganda shit and you ain't never been here before?"

As they talked, it occurred to me that a little time with Armando might be the best medicine for Martin. The only question—how to arrange it? I thought briefly of my own session with Armando the day before. In the nude he was a stunning sight—a chest that curved like a shield, an ass as dazzling as mother-of-pearl. Best of all, Armando had no inhibitions in bed.

I lay back on the blanket, closing my eyes. The sun streamed orange through my eyelids. Yes, a session with Armando was just what Martin needed. But there was a problem of money.

After showering yesterday, Armando had fried himself two eggs in olive oil and washed them down with Pepsi. As he was leaving, I stuffed a ten dollar bill in his shirt pocket. My delicacy had been misplaced. He took out the bill, looked at it, then gave me a big Chiclet smile and departed whistling.

I sat up suddenly. "Martin, how about buying us a beer?"

He accepted the coins somewhat peevishly, unfolded his long body from the blanket and trudged to the beach bar. From the rear, his thin neck and peaked shoulders reminded me of a large stork.

I turned to Armando. "Martin likes you, I can tell." I paused, embarrassed. Pimping wasn't exactly my line. "He needs some ... uh ... relaxation."

Armando raised his massive eyebrows but said nothing.

"He's a gay liberationist. Gay liberationists don't ... like to pay. It's sort of ... against their principles."

"Well, see, I gotta lotta problems right now. My sister, she ..."

I cut him off. "I'll give you something. See, I want Martin to have a good time."

Armando turned to look at Martin, a white sliver against the blaze of noon. "You sure you know this guy?" he asked.

Martin seemed even more irritated when he came back. "The United States wants Puerto Rico as a captive market for exports," he said, handing Armando a Budweiser. Armando tossed back his head as he drank it. His adam's apple was strong and corded. "Sit down," he said to Martin, "here." He smoothed a place beside him. As Martin sank down, Armando brushed his hand lightly across his shoulders. Martin seemed to quiver all over, then pushed back his glasses and began to talk about mercantilism.

"I'm going to take a walk," I announced a few minutes later, but they didn't seem to hear. When I came back, I found the blanket unoccupied. I sat down, trying not to feel exultant. I waited a good hour before going upstairs.

I rang the apartment bell before entering, but I needn't have. Armando, his powerful body draped in a yellow towel, was looking at a pamphlet entitled *The Homophile Rights Movement in Germany*. Martin, in baggy underwear, was frying eggs in olive oil. The smile he gave me seemed to hurt his facial muscles. I had the impression of ice breaking up in spring.

"Well, well," I said, oozing false heartiness, "look who's here."

"We waited, but you was gone," Armando observed.

"So I was."

Martin served up the eggs with two Pepsi-Colas. I left them eating side by side.

Armando came into the bathroom as I was drying off after a shower. He didn't bother to knock. He stood in front of the toilet and unleashed a thick stream of urine. He hadn't been trained to aim at the porcelain side; it sounded like the Horseshoe Falls.

"Your friend," he nodded toward the door, *"buena gente."*

"Martin?" I stifled a slight pang of jealousy. *Buena gente* was a true compliment in Puerto Rico—somewhere between *nice guy* and *solid citizen*. Armando had never applied the term to me.

"I gotta get goin' now," Armando announced. I knew what he was getting at. I gave him a slight nod, full of conspiracy, and told him to wait for me on the terrace. I slipped him the ten dollars a few minutes later. He palmed it while glancing over his shoulder. Martin was washing the dishes.

At the door, Martin held out his hands to Armando. *"Hasta la vista,"* he murmured. His face seemed softer, less pinched. For the first time he looked younger rather than older—perhaps no more than thirty.

"Hasta la vista, friend," Armando's dark eyes glittered. Then he hugged Martin, gave me a pleasant nod, and departed. Martin sat for a long time afterward, still in his underwear, looking at the ocean without speaking.

We were on the terrace that evening, watching the sunset, when Martin brought the subject up. "You see," he said, "they don't want to be prostitutes. The system makes them."

I nodded. The daiquiri was pungent on my lips.

"It's the death culture," he went on.

I nodded again. The sun was half gone. I could almost feel the earth turn.

"Imperialism is dying," he observed, turning his back to the horizon. I watched the last glowing fingernail disappear. "I'm meeting Armando tomorrow," he continued. "He's taking me to La Perla."

I lowered my drink. "La Perla!"

"I told him I read *La Vida.* You know, by Oscar Lewis..."

"I know it's by Oscar Lewis," I snapped.

"And I want to see firsthand how the poor people live."

I reached for the daiquiri pitcher, trying to hide my irritation. I didn't really understand it. I had no desire to visit the city's worst slum, yet the thought of Martin and Armando there... My irritation thickened, followed by guilt. Wasn't this exactly what I wanted for Martin? Wasn't his visit becoming a success—instantly, and beyond my wildest hopes?

Armando turned up next morning, wearing a purple T-shirt that said *Puerto Rico Me Encanta.* Martin greeted him with a shy smile and a kiss on the cheek. They held hands for a long moment.

"You gonna let me drive the car?" Armando demanded.

I had made up my mind the night before—no car for the

visit to La Perla. "If you drive *very* carefully," I heard myself say.

"Man, like it was my own." He seemed to know where I kept the keys—in the bureau in the bedroom. As they left—Martin's face pink with sun and excitement—I had to restrain myself from slamming the door behind them.

When I came back from the beach around four, I found them in bed with the door open. It looked as if they had been there for some time.

"How was La Perla?" I asked.

They told me all about it—the tattoo artists, fortunetellers, prostitutes, junkies. "Armando met an old woman who knew his father," Martin giggled. Lying in bed, cradled in Armando's dark arms, he looked even younger than yesterday. It occurred to me that the years were shredding away. "Papa could still get it up when he was seventy-two. Armando says he was a ... um ..."

"*Jodedor!*" Armando yowled. "Means big fucker. My father was the famous fucker from Manatí!"

They both roared at that, turning toward each other. I swiveled quickly and went into the bathroom. As I turned on the water I heard their laughter soften and disappear. I closed the door. I didn't want to hear what came next.

Armando made his pitch while I was fixing myself a rum coco.

"I spent a lotta *chabo* today," he shook his head.

"Yeah?"

He didn't notice my unsympathetic tone. "We give a kid something, he was on crutches, like that. I bought these beads from an *espiritista*. She say my Saint Geronimo will take care of me now."

I scowled. "Geronimo wasn't a saint. He was an Indian chief."

"I know that, man." His voice was plaintive. "Now I'm broke. *Pelado.*"

The rum coco was ready. I poured it into a ceramic glass shaped like a frog. I could hear Martin singing in the shower.

7

"You told me you wanted him to have a good time." Armando's voice was accusing.

"Yeah, I did."

"So?"

I couldn't explain it—not to myself, certainly not to Armando. All I knew was that I was trapped in Martin Chrisman's view of things. In his dream world. It was no consolation to know that I was paying the rent on the goddam place myself.

"Here," I thrust the ten dollars at him angrily. He looked at me with large sad eyes, then put it away, shaking his head.

As the days went by, Martin changed more and more. He seemed to straighten up, fill more of the space around him. He and Armando spent long hours playing dominoes, howling with glee at every silly move. They traded necklaces of cowrie shells in a little ceremony in which they pledged eternal brotherhood. Martin shopped for and cooked a traditional Puerto Rican *asopao,* using a recipe Armando's mother supplied.

When he was alone with me, however, he trotted out his lectures on Puerto Rican politics. I went along with his theories, holding my tongue, giving place. Armando had been hitting me for ten dollars every day.

But my self-control reached the breaking point on the last evening of Martin's visit. We had had a lovely day at Luquillo, a superb beach an hour's drive from San Juan. Armando had borrowed some spear-fishing gear and snagged a couple of red snappers. We brought them home and got ready for a big evening.

Armando was on the terrace grilling the fish when the argument started in the kitchen.

"There's only one solution to the political situation here," Martin said. His face was tanned now, the seams all smoothed out. He might have been in his early twenties. "We have to start a guerrilla operation in the rain forest. Like in Cuba—the Sierra Maestra." He glanced toward the terrace. Armando was flipping the fish. "Violence is the only solution."

I stared at him in disbelief. "Do you realize that the Puerto Ricans always vote twenty to one *against* cutting their ties to the U.S.?"

He shook his head smugly, maddeningly. "Doesn't matter. They have to be educated. Have their political consciousness raised. Ask Armando. He agrees with me."

"Armando..." I started to say, thinking about Armando's reverence for most things American.

"Now," Martin read my thoughts. "He agrees with me *now."* The smug look intensified. "I've educated him."

Suddenly I couldn't hold back any more. Everything I had refrained from saying for the past seven days took shape on the tip of my tongue. "How do you know Armando doesn't like being a colonial?" My voice was hoarse, unfamiliar. "Doesn't like being exploited?"

Martin looked at me and I read triumph in his brown eyes. "Did he ask me for money?" He threw back his head and whinnied. "Did he?"

It was infuriating. I could feel all my good intentions dissolving in a brew of anger. "No," I said slowly, nailing down the words, "but how do you know he didn't ask me?"

That stopped him. His face straightened and his eyes focused into fearful points behind his glasses. "Because..." he said at last, "he wouldn't... do such... a thing." His shoulders hunched and for a moment he seemed terribly young and vulnerable. "He... isn't... capable of it," he whispered.

I stood up, caught between anger and shame, while Martin stared at the floor. My head was buzzing. Hardly aware of my movements, I headed for the terrace. I knew the sight of the sea would cool me, stop the buzzing in my head, give me a chance to think.

Armando said something but I stepped around him, unhearing, and went to the rail. The waters stretched away, velvety and black, as far as I could see. Why hadn't I told Martin the truth, the whole truth? Why had I allowed the dream, the lie, to stand? The answer came to me on the silken murmur of a palm frond, stirred by the sea wind. I *wanted* Martin to believe the world was full of true love. I *wanted* him to believe it was about to be reformed. His idealism—absurd, misplaced—sustained me. I needed it as much as he did.

The evening ended drunkenly. Martin stripped to his baggy drawers and sang a Spanish song that Armando had taught him. He seemed to have turned into someone else entirely. When I stumbled out, around midnight, they were sitting on the floor and Martin was stroking Armando's hair gently.

IT WAS THE following spring that I ran into Armando in Times Square. He was slumped inside a dirty sweater. He looked like the survivor of a city under siege.

"Hey, man!" I saw the ghost of a Chiclet smile.

"Armando! How are you?"

He told me he had arrived in New York a month earlier. He hadn't been able to find work. "I'm broke," he said. *"Pelado."*

The words had a horrible familiarity, and I started to step aside. But I checked myself. "Seen Martin?" I asked.

"Yeah, all the time."

A pang of jealousy assailed me. "Why not ask Martin to help you?"

Armando shook his head. "I never ask Martin for nothin'. He don't go for that shit." He paused. "All he got is beautiful ideas."

I snorted. "Ideas about what?"

"About life, man, *life.*" He straightened up suddenly and jabbed a left hook into the air. It seemed an absurd bit of bravado on 42nd Street. Perhaps he realized it too, because he slumped again. "Can you gimme something?" he asked. "I'll pay you back."

I shook my head sharply, angrily, but then reached for my wallet. He took the bill between fingers that were gray and dirty. He didn't even thank me. Just turned away, avoiding my eyes, while he gave me a peace salute. "Stay cool," he murmured.

I don't know how long I stood there, watching his bowed head disappear through the swarms of people. But I moved on at last, cursing Martin Chrisman under my breath as I realized I would forever be a prisoner of his stupidity, his simplicity, his love.

The Taste of Spring

I RECEIVED THE phone call yesterday. They have offered me ten thousand dollars for the letters. It seems a high price, but Howard tells me that the University of Texas frequently pays more for literary documents. In fact, he suggested that I hold out for a higher sum. This was over breakfast, the sun streaking the kitchen floor, teasing us with its brightness. It is too early for real warmth, of course. March in New Hampshire is a brittle joke. But still, it may be warm enough for leaf-raking, later. I wonder if I will have the strength for my big garden this year. Winter has drained me; no other winter has seemed so hard.

Howard wants me to respond to his idea. We are waiting for the waffle iron to heat up—it takes forever—and he watches me. I see the nonchalant look that attends the discussion of money.

"I'd ask twelve thousand, mother," he says. His face, poised over the edge of his cup, is puffy with sleep. He came over from Durham—he teaches there—last night. In another hour his face will refine itself into its usual hard-edged alertness.

"How did they hear about the letters?" I ask. "I wish they wouldn't bother me with these things." I try not to sound petulant.

"For God's sake, someone offers you a small fortune and you wish they hadn't?"

He sees it so simply—money in exchange for property. Older people's passions do not exist for the young. But perhaps I am being unfair. Howard has a nice sense of the past, considering he is a history teacher.

I watch him—his nose is a perfect hypotenuse—and know I cannot explain it over breakfast. I think of the pachysandra outside, eternally green. Its root system is a thick mat of fibers, grasping and hairy. It requires great patience to trace it to its furthest points. Most people, when they transplant pachysandra in the spring, chop at the roots with a trowel. I do not want to uproot Alma's letters by chopping at them that way. On the other hand, I do not have the patience to trace their ramifications.

The waffle irons are ready at last. Howard has been lifting the lids every few seconds, letting the heat escape.

"Would you mind telling me what your objections are, exactly?"

"Well," I rummage around for an excuse. "I don't know what they'd do with them."

"What they always do with manuscripts. Display them. Let researchers use them. Publish them." I suppose I looked pained, because he added, "What's wrong with that?"

"Nothing."

"Well?"

More simplification. But perhaps it is not my own lack of patience or Howard's greed that upsets me. There are other fears. Suddenly I wish he would hurry up and finish. I want to go outside. I might learn more about the letters by taking a walk on my land, over the three bridges to the farthest field, which Howard once dubbed the Happy Valley. The sunlight is so tempting. I forget that it is only an illusion of spring.

But he is eating slowly. Two, four, six waffles. I can see that he is wrestling with another idea. His face is glowing with nonchalance; he must be thinking of money again.

"You know, mother, if you don't want Texas to have the letters now..." he reaches for more butter, disguising his discomfort, "... you could leave them the damn things in your will. That way they won't be lost to posterity. After all, you have some kind of responsibility, Alma Maitland..." He shrugs and a thin, insincere smile appears.

He is on the verge of simony, meanest sin in the catalogue. My children know that my will is already written, a strict and direful document dividing everything *per stirpes*. He need only wait, and the letters will belong to him and Gloria. But of course he is afraid. He doesn't trust me. He believes I will destroy them. Perhaps he sees me more truthfully, more nakedly, than I see myself. No doubt he has glimpsed the privacy, like a deep screen at my center, which still enfolds Alma and myself. He fears it because it has nothing to do with him or his sister. Their egotism which, I confess, I have nurtured, rejects the notion that my life might contain something to which they cannot be admitted.

"What do you think of that? In your will?"

I know what he will say if I agree. He will suggest that the letters be put somewhere safe, in our attorney's office, or in a lockbox to which only he has the key. But I have outguessed him.

"I'm going for a walk," I say flatly, leaving him openmouthed, holding a forkful of waffle.

The sun greets me coldly but the sky is beautiful. I search it for some recognition that I have come through my sixtieth year with my teeth and my mercy intact. I take a deep breath and the air rushes into my lungs, stabbing me. I see the leaves under the laurel and hemlock—not the piebald nuggets of autumn but the dead sad leaves of spring. I think momentarily of my own deep winter's fatigue. Then I remember Howard. His life, since Sue left him, taking Jonathan, aged four, has the sadness of the leaves. I turn some clusters with my foot. When I come back from my walk, I will rake a little, if I am not too tired.

Some people call these my woods, but they are not. I do not own these trees; I merely have a lifetime lien on them. I am not part of their future triumph. When I reach the second bridge, halfway back on my hundred acres, I find that the watercress has surfaced. Watercress! It seems too early, but there it is, waving its snaky stems in water thick and bright as Baccarat crystal. Of course, I must eat some right away, kneeling down on the flat wooden boards, the pebbles hurting my knees while I pile the long crisp strands into my mouth. Their iciness stings my lips and teeth but I persist. It is a ritual moment, the eating of spring.

It is there, my lips numb and the tartness burning my tongue, that I have a sudden view of Alma. She is standing on the topmost step leading to Sacré-Cœur, its three domes rising behind her like halved onions, laughing. "Ten thousand dollars so the professors can read about the summer I cut off your hair with a straight razor?"

And then her face—she had a small face, with the skin stretched so tightly you thought you were seeing bone—formed into a smile and I realized that she liked the nonsense of it. She had a fine sense of nonsense, Alma did. She never became outraged or aggrieved when people said harsh things about her books. She would become thoughtful and her eyes would dance sideways, as if looking for a place to land, then change the subject. Recrimination was not her specialty. She had a fine distance from things, which never turned into dryness.

"Yes, Alma," I almost said, "can you imagine?"

But of course, she could. Imagining was her trade, followed by the setting down in exact detail. I thought of her first description of Madeleine. "She was tall and uncertain, as if she had suffered from years of poor kissing."

The words made my skin quiver now, although it might have been the cold edging up my parka sleeves. I look at the watercress, holding fast against the crystal current. Quickly, before I can regret it, I plunge in my hands and tear off two nests. We will have it for dinner. It is hard carrying the greens without gloves but I won't let myself flinch. Alma taught me two things: to tell the truth and never to flinch.

I met her at a musical evening at the home of the Princesse de Scay, in one of those great rose palaces on the Avenue Foch. Alma appeared beside me in the dining room after the music was over, a taut woman shorter than I by almost a head.

"You have been in Paris since when?" I was surprised by the French construction since she was American, but I liked her voice. Later I found that she always spoke with great precision as if, in picking her way through countless shades of meaning, she had settled on surfaces as the most reliable of all.

"Just a month."

"You have friends here?"

"A few." I didn't tell her that I had only one close friend, Jean Hartman, a vague fat girl who entertained students from the medical school around the corner and had an absurd crush on Cécile Sorel.

"Then you must make more."

When I told her about my room, astir all night with mice, she clicked her tongue disapprovingly. "We will find you a better place to live," she said.

"But I like it there!" I burst out. It wasn't true and she knew it. I was quite lost in Paris until Alma took me up. I might just as well have been back in Ohio.

In the dining room of the Princesse de Scay's *hôtel particulier,* under the Sert ceiling, we stood side by side, speaking our flat syllables and probing for each other's outline underneath, trying to get a fix on something we could not quite see. At the time, I was aware of: her white face, the taste of champagne, an irresistible urge to laugh. It all seemed very dangerous and correct at the same time. The other guests, rushing past us toward the buffet, reminded me of pigs feeding at a trough. They lapped up the food noisily, not giving place. Perhaps they thought it was their reward for having sat through two hours of Monteverdi and Gesualdo and Stravinsky on straight-backed chairs. We watched them with dismay. Or rather, I watched them. Alma watched me. Another line from the book comes back to me now: "We stood apart from the rest, engulfed in the future; suddenly it seemed a useless thing not to be in love."

I thought no one had observed us, but when we left, the Princesse de Scay, ruthless in blue tulle and a hairdo like a brioche, leaned over the stairwell and hissed at me, "Be careful, my dear, that one is a thief of souls."

I laughed too loudly, and felt awkward as we collected our wraps downstairs.

Since the watercress is numbing my hands, I hasten my steps toward the house. I can see it in the distance, white with black shutters and a yellow trim. There is a gravestone in the backyard, marking the grave of a child who died in 1839. I have made a bench from it—I don't think that is disrespectful.

This morning Howard told me that I have been mentioned in some of the biographies of Alma Maitland that are appearing—it is the season for biographies—and that *The Rainbow Dance* is thought to be the finest of her novels. He said they never discuss it without a reference to me, the model for Madeleine. How Alma would have loved the solemn foolishness of that! As I climb the last rise and stop in full view of the house, I remember the morning following our first meeting, when we walked through the Bois while a light spring snow fell. The flakes melted on our lips with the elusive texture of a soufflé.

Alma was wise enough not to hurry me. We spent several months in each other's company before she touched me. By then I was aching with curiosity and fear. She knew I was ready by the way I sat next to her on the sofa. Some friends from Cleveland had just departed. We shared that snugness that comes when two people remain after a party. No doubt I was giving off signals, like a star. She cupped her hand under my chin and brought my face up. Then she grazed my lips delicately with hers. I had the taste of something crisp and tart. The last thing I saw, closing my eyes, was her face like a blossom.

I believe a great deal has recently been written about the act of love between women, although I have read none of it. I am not interested. Other women can transmit nothing of their experience to me. I can only remember Alma.

First, let me say that after she kissed me, everything slowed down, as if the clocks in the room had lost interest in ticking and the flowers in withering. She undressed me slowly, folding each garment after she removed it. I do not, strangely, remember the physical part now, except to recall that her body was astonishingly white. Oh yes, one other thing—the scent. Alma never used perfume but the room that evening was tinged with the odor of May-lily. The odor seemed to exist in bands; if I turned one way I could smell it, another way, not.

And I could not stop laughing. How silly that sounds now. But as we came together, our legs elongating so that the bones clicked, a surge of laughter started, as if a hundred goldfinches were loose in the cage of my ribs. How funny it was! And how much came out in that laughter! My mother, corseted in eternal black. My father, fat and kind and avaricious. Both of them stepping out of their second tombs, the ones they occupied in my memory. How grateful they should have been to Alma for that laughter!

Inside the kitchen, I put the watercress to soak. My hands are blocks of ice but I cannot resist a last nibble. Amazing that these vines should bring back so many other tastes—the champagne served by the Princesse de Scay, the snow in the Bois, Alma's kisses. Then I know why I left Howard at the waffle iron this morning. The watercress was calling, notifying me it had survived the winter.

HOWARD IS NOWHERE to be seen. Perhaps he has gone out for a walk too. I put on the *Emperor* Concerto and sit on the couch, while Sukie, my seven-toed cat, climbs crossly on my lap. On the album cover, Beethoven is ferocious with jut jaw and woolly-bear eyebrows. In the bow of his head I see not sullen defeat but a surrender to terrible necessities.

Yes. I moved to New Hampshire after Lyman died. At the time, Howard was in the Army, Gloria was getting a business degree at Columbia. I was tired of life in New York City, tired of our apartment, doubtful about taking a job. It seemed more likely that the countryside would hold me. I would raise sheep or start a mail-order business or farm my own land. As it turned out, I did all three. New Hampshire seemed just right. Brief, orgiastic summers and ironbound winters. Both seemed necessary to keep me in equilibrium. I would have some cats for company.

I was not shattered when Lyman died, although you must not think I failed to love him. We had twenty good years. There was an imperturbability to him—perhaps it came from working all day with numbers—that made life with him easy. I told Lyman about Alma before we were married. It seemed fair. I think he saw Alma merely as an escapade, part of Getting Ready For Life. He smiled as he listened, but a shadow hovered around his eyes.

After the children were born, I almost never thought of her, although I read that she had returned to America, and was living not far from us. I made no effort to see her. It would have exaggerated the past, and I was buried in the present.

The first movement of the Beethoven concerto ends and suddenly I know what I have to do. Sweeping Sukie from my lap, I go upstairs to hunt for the keys to the safe-deposit box.

Backing the car out, I have the sense that another woman is at the wheel. Alma's letters have been in the box at the savings bank since I moved north. While housecleaning after Lyman's funeral, I discovered them at the bottom of a sack full of photographs. I had moved them to the country with me, putting them in the lockbox along with the stocks and deeds and insurance policies. Why did I decide, then, to take care of them, after years of not bothering? I could not answer that, then or now.

I park the car in the grocery-store lot across from the bank, as if my errand were best camouflaged, even from myself. As I walk past the tellers' cages toward the vault, I give only the briefest good mornings. I hope no one will notice me, or stop to chat.

The letters are at the back of the box, in a thick sheaf tied by cotton string that is greasy and black. I cram them into my purse and hurry out, looking straight ahead. Driving home, I take them out and hold them on my lap. They feel heavy against my thighs.

HOWARD HAS BEEN on a mysterious errand all day. His little car turns into the driveway an hour before sunset. He gives me a jovial greeting that makes me wonder. Perhaps he has a woman friend somewhere. His euphoria accompanies him like a cloud as he mixes a martini.

We have dinner on the glassed-in back porch, watching the early robins hop about, listening for the silken rustle of earthworms. But it grows cold so we decide to have coffee in the parlor. The room has a certain stiffness to it, Howard claims, and he is right. But to me, it's a good stiffness, the kind that comes of straight backs and feet on the floor. A stiffness that counters the slippages of the flesh.

Howard looks very handsome on the loveseat, his skin honey-colored in the firelight. I supposes he uses his pipe to posture a bit. I wonder again about the woman friend, then think about Sue and Jonathan. He has not discussed his wife's departure much. Sitting here, I realize how little I know about my son. I have allowed my former acquaintance with his body to console me for my ignorance of his life.

At last Howard taps his pipe into the milky palms of an ashtray. He is elaborately casual about this, and I know he has an unpleasant announcement to make. Then, in a flash of recognition, I know he has no woman friend. I have misjudged him, out of my own need. His euphoria stems from a mean satisfaction of some kind.

"I think you're going to be a little annoyed." He glances at me mildly. His hair is a tawny puff on his forehead. "I've been to see Alma Maitland."

I stare at him, my ears roaring.

"She lives in Greenwich Village. On Milligan Place." He studies his hands. "The meeting was arranged by her publisher."

I sit back, clasping my hands together, looking at him. My man-child. He is thirty-two years old. *It was Howard who told the university about the letters!* I have not transferred the most important things to him. Is it possible I wanted to keep them all to myself? I think of the watercress, and fight the urge to run outside, into the desolate March night.

"There's nothing in the letters about her novel, Howard. Nothing." I am surprised at the evenness of my voice.

"But you were corresponding with her that year. The year you came home, the year she was writing the book."

I shake my head. He doesn't understand. Perhaps part of me, one translucent plate of me, had been in the character of Madeleine. But Howard is looking for the wrong object.

"What the professors are collecting," I murmur, "is not authors. Not books. They're collecting passions. Fine old passions." My eyes go to the Delftware on the mantel. "Sort of . . . a china that doesn't belong to them."

He makes an impatient move and bites his lips. "That's absurd."

"Of course. Men and women without passions of their own are always absurd."

He takes the pipe from his mouth. "Don't you want to hear what Alma Maitland said?"

I shake my head, but he goes on.

"She wants to see you. She won't make a decision about the letters until she talks to you."

I shake my head again, this time angrily. "But the letters are mine!"

"Physically. But the contents are hers. The words. They belong to her and her literary heirs forever."

"Then why . . ."

"Because if you sell the letters, mother..." he spaces out the words, "... they still need her permission to publish."

"But I told you, the letters have no literary value. They're personal!"

"I asked her about that," he replies silkily. "She said she was thinking about you when she wrote. The letters are part of the whole creative process. They kept you alive in her mind."

He looks at me and shifts uncomfortably.

"You know, Mother," his nonchalance is oppressive now, "if you're embarrassed about.. well, about all that... you needn't be. Things have changed. In fact, those days in Paris, when all those famous..." His face grows flushed. He seems to be choking.

"Lesbians," I explain softly. "They were famous lesbians. Women who needed women."

He looks relieved, although he does not lift his eyes to mine. "Yes. That's part of, well, cultural history. Gertrude Stein, Radclyffe Hall, Natalie Barney... they're getting a lot of attention now." He names some books. They sound terribly insignificant.

The princes of the blood, Alma used to call them. But they were not royal or grand. They were merely enigmatic, from having made love the center of their lives. How could those figures be rendered into lines on a page? The professors would try to explain, justify, harmonize—find patterns where none existed.

Howard clears his throat. "I went ahead and set up a date for you and Alma to get together. We can clear all this up."

"You did all that without asking me?"

"I set it up for Monday. Day after tomorrow. I called school and canceled my classes so I can go with you."

How extraordinary he is, he and the other professors.

"Mother." His voice is low, pleading. "It's a terrific chance for me."

He wants to write something for one of the history journals. It will help his reputation. As he explains, I wonder what he would say if he knew the letters were upstairs in the secret compartment of my bureau. Would he steal them while I slept?

Six o'clock Sunday morning. The huge Norway pine outside my window whispers me awake. I lie in the dark, visualizing the road. I won't bother with breakfast, for fear of waking Howard.

As I step outside, the day lies at my feet in an accusing crouch. Why am I leaving, with the raking undone, the crocus shoots uncovered? What can possibly compensate for these duties overlooked? Can the letters, now protruding from my coat pocket? Or meeting Alma again? There is a caesura in my life, a breach between the time with Alma and today. Is it senility that makes me want to leap backward in time, over that breach?

Alone on the road, I keep the needle at seventy. My thoughts probe at Howard. Six months ago he arrived home from his afternoon class to find a note from Sue. She had gone, taking Jonathan. No forwarding address, no separation proceedings, no request for support. She had simply melted away, unforgiving, unforgiven. I have a glimpse of Sue making her decision: her brown eyes deep, her sinewy hands knotted as her woman's resiliency tells her she will be better nourished elsewhere. Where are you, Sue? It is a question I throw to a woodchuck, scrawny in his winter underwear, beside the road. I have the sudden notion that Sue is in California, at the rim of the continent, finding the place in her marked No Farther.

And what of Howard, my son? My errand today will turn him against me, at least for a while. Why didn't I let that stop me? The truth is that nothing can stop me, not placating Howard nor tending my yard. I am in the grip of a force as implacable as spring.

As I reach the outskirts of New York, I realize I don't know Alma's exact address. Milligan Place has more than a dozen houses.

She is in the last one, of course, the name in broken block letters above the bell. It is ten o'clock; Greenwich Village has the stillness of a country churchyard.

I ring the bell once, twice, annoyed at myself for not having planned this in advance. But after the third ring, there is an answering buzz. I step inside the house, which tilts crazily. It seems to be sliding to the right. I hear a querulous voice overhead.

As I reply, "A friend," I recall a picture of Alma on the jacket of *The Rainbow Dance*. I wish I had not, because the image is full of pain, but—pulling myself upstairs—it comes back, insisting, until it is perfect in every detail. Alma sits in a carved wooden chair, her legs crossed carelessly. She is wearing a soft felt hat with the brim turned down, a Chanel suit, high heels. A cloth coat is draped carelessly around her shoulders. It is the picture of a young woman who has no quarrel with the foolery of the world, a woman who has understood everything and agreed to pretend that she has not.

I hear moist, impatient noises as I climb the last flight. I am afraid to look up. The photograph hammers at me.

A small pale woman with thin hair is peering at me. Her eyes are faded, her figure raddled under the cotton housedress. I straighten up, catching my breath. I can see no resemblance to the photograph.

"I asked who you are," she snaps. Her voice is pocked with age.

I stand there, still tracing the photograph. Surely somewhere...

"Why don't you answer me?"

"I'm sorry, Alma."

The faded blue eyes quicken. "Oh, it's you." She puts one hand to her throat and I see veins like brown tendrils. Then she motions to the open door behind her.

The apartment is almost bare. She does not offer to take my coat. "You needn't look around much," she says, "there's nothing here."

I stand, waiting. After a moment, she says, "Your son says

you want to sell the letters." Her mouth stretches into an angry pleat. "Why did you keep them? They weren't to be kept."

For answer, I remove the packet and hold it out. It takes a moment for her eyes to focus. Then she accepts it and motions to an armless wooden chair. She sits across from me, clasping the letters with both hands. Our eyes meet and for the first time something passes between us. I recognize it as an absurd desire to laugh. And then I understand why I kept the letters all these years, why I removed them from the lockbox, why I came here today. My breath, still short from climbing the stairs, whispers the truth. The motes dancing in front of my eyes confirm it. The letters are the link between the outer edges of my life, the times of testing. Proof that as I had the strength to be young, I shall have the strength to be old. The early spring will see me through the late.

Suddenly I see the ghost of a smile on Alma's face. "Publishing scoundrels," she giggles.

"Parasites," I murmur. Then louder, "Collectors of other people's china."

She holds up the letters. Her face has softened. For an instant I imagine she is wearing a felt hat with the brim turned down. Then she smiles at me—sweetly, imperiously. My laughter slips out and fills the space between us.

She rises and comes toward me. As I taste spring on my lips again I realize that Howard and the professors have disappeared without a trace into the eternal winter of middle age.

Colors

THREE OF US were sitting around the table in the small wooden house. José Antonio had been drinking the most, pouring himself swallows of rum, slowing down as the liquor took effect. Hector and I watched. There was no reason to talk, just as there was no reason to discourage José from drinking. We had accepted his hospitality and we had to stay. In another hour he might be ready. The rum, the tides, the rising moon—maybe even his aunt Tata pounding yautía dough in the kitchen—would combine to loosen his tongue. But not yet. Once or twice he turned his head and by the light of the kerosene lamp I could see moisture trapped under his eyes, glistening on the dark skin. And he murmured his friend's name once or twice. "Lindo." A pause, then again, "Lindo."

Hector and I looked at each other from time to time. I don't know what he was thinking, but I knew my own mind: it was filled with regret. We had regressed a century in just an afternoon, from the sleek designer world of the Caribe Hilton to this gloomy town locked in a mangrove swamp, laid out on a grid of streets called Número Uno, Número Dos, Número Tres. A town inhabited by dark and listless young men with nothing to do but stand around and watch the cars go by. Not a hotel, not a supermarket—nothing but tiny cafés and unsanitary-looking groceries, where coconuts were piled up like so many human skulls and the smoke of charcoal fires carried the sickly-sweet smell of frying alcapurrias through the air. Nothing but decay and drowsiness and heat like a cargo of coals. Earlier today we had driven along the coast road from San Juan and I'd glimpsed an elementary school with broken shutters, a U.S. post office with its flag in tatters, a dead cat bloated with maggots. Shocking displays of communal indifference or laziness—but Hector didn't seem to notice and I kept my disgust to myself. I was a guest on his beloved island. Besides, we'd driven out to attend the fiesta, and he was in a holiday mood.

We parked half a mile from the center of town. The place was jammed with cars, nosed into yards, vacant lots, the beach. Hector locked up carefully and set the burglar alarm. Then we joined the stream of tourists.

It wasn't much of a fiesta by European standards. If you've seen the feria in Seville or the Palio in Siena, and then you turn up at the Fiesta de Santiago Apóstol in this grubby little coastal village, you're in for a shock. There's nothing but a few maskers, a few floats, a little excitement when the statue of St. James goes by—and that's it. Where, you wonder, are the pageantry, the pomp, the memory of great events? There's nothing really but heat and flies and poverty.

And rum. Hector and I wandered through the crowd, going from one little palm hut to another. *"Un palito,"* Hector would say to a smiling man the color of mahogany, and he'd pour some Don Q into a paper cup. *"Salud,"* Hector would murmur, and toss it off. He was sweating a lot but wouldn't stop drinking, wouldn't move to the shade. I finally left him and stood under a giant *flamboyán,* its upper stories ablaze with blossoms. I watched from there.

After the statue of the saint went by, the high school band passed, then some elderly ladies dressed in white. Then the first of the maskers roared in. They were men dressed as medieval knights, with white and pink masks that made them look strangely out of place in that dark crowd. They ran around the square making passes at the girls while everybody whooped. After a while another group appeared—men in grotesque horned masks and long, colorful gowns. These were the *vejigantes,* someone told me—evil spirits. They ran around too, and as I watched their silly antics I felt myself yearning for my air-conditioned room at the Hilton. Hector had disappeared, the July heat was like a mailed fist and the rum was making me sleepy.

The next minute I was wide awake. *"Las mujeres locas!"* a fat woman in yellow slacks roared, holding up her son to see. A line of men in drag—big, hulking fishermen and construction workers wearing kerchiefs and skirts—appeared. They were hugely funny, their tits slipped into weird shapes, their asses padded with pillows. At one point they paired off and did a mad fandango around the plaza while the crowd went wild and the kids imitated them. When they finished dancing, they started asking for money, ganging up on people who wouldn't pay and knocking into them with their bosoms. One well-dressed tourist got chased around until he reached his car and dove in, locking the doors.

I ran into Hector right after the drag act had disappeared towards the beach. He was sitting on the steps of the stone church, its hide as wrinkled and gray as an elephant's, talking to a big dark man. He hailed me over and introduced me.

"José used to be one of the *locas*," Hector said, waving in the direction of the beach.

José looked at me and curved his dark hands over his chest. "I got *tetas* like you never see on no woman," he said. There was something strong, almost menacing, about the statement, and I managed an appreciative nod.

"My mother was a *mantenedora*," he added.

"Means she took care of the statue of the saint," Hector explained.

"You see it?" José asked.

I had, the saint on a white horse, a raised silver sword in his hand, the head of a Moor under the horse's hooves. The float that carried it had been pulled by half a dozen men.

"Nobody take care of the saint like my mother," José went on, pressing his fists together—they were big as boxing gloves. "After she die, they give it to another woman. They never let a man take care of the saint." He turned his head away, and I sensed some kind of pain, then dismissed it.

As if to confirm my impression of strength, José stood up. He was huge, monumental, like one of those statues that stand in socialist squares with names like Worker or Wheat or Machinery. His features, under his dark skin, were sharp, almost Indian. I reminded myself that the Tainos had lived here long before the slave ships landed. He looked at me and smiled.

"I want you come to my house," he said. He gestured toward the beach. "We have a drink of rum."

I started to say I'd had enough rum, but José had moved close to me—close with that special intimacy of Latins who don't believe in much space between people. I could smell him, a yeasty mixture of sweat and vegetation, and see the short wiry hairs, like tiny springs, below his throat. I looked to Hector for rescue, but Hector was smiling. "José wants to tell you his story," he said.

José was almost pushing against me now. I had the impression he might knock me down, then sit on me, apologizing profusely.

"What kind of story?" I took a few steps back, but José followed.

"A story about New York. He thinks you oughta hear it."

José took my forearm. His palm was slick and papery. "You come, mister," he said. I agreed reluctantly and we headed for the car.

José's house was a wooden cottage on stilts, buried in a bamboo grove. Other similar houses stood nearby. Through the bamboo I could see the ocean and hear the soft licking sound of water. The central room of the cottage contained a table and some chairs and a platform with a stained mattress. José's aunt Tata, an ancient black woman with José's aquiline features, shuffled in. Later I heard her pounding on a wooden block in the back.

José produced a bottle of rum and found some glasses. He and Hector sat at the rickety table, but I moved to the mattress and began to smoke, to keep the mosquitoes at bay.

The drinking had gone on for an hour when José finally began. By then I was half asleep, the dampness that had seeped into my jeans forgotten, even the mosquitoes ignored. The rum had smoothed me out, pressed me into a dreamy state which made it easy for me to understand José's Spanish. I didn't even have to translate—the words just drifted from his spirit to mine, without benefit of a dictionary. I set them down here in English, as best I recall, reminding you that Spanish is a flowery and overdramatic tongue—perhaps it is the Arab influence—and that José, once he got going, spun out the phrases like a storyteller in an African market-town. Perhaps he fabricated the whole tale, or perhaps I dreamed it in that bamboo grove in a dark and forgotten corner of the world. I don't know. But here it is. You can judge for yourself how much, if any of it, is true.

YOU LIVE IN NEW YORK (he began) and that is where it all ended. But it started right here in our village, which was founded by black men who preferred their own people in the swamps to the white people in the cities. Oh, they begged us to leave, begged us to come and work for them now that our chains were broken and the Law of Abolition had liberated thirty thousand men and women. But we knew better. We knew we belonged here where the white egrets nest at night and the gray pitirre sings in the morning. Where there would be no pale Irish planters to drive us out to the canefields, no creole ladies with bright skin and whirling fans, no Yankee soldiers with ice-blue eyes and selfish mouths. Yes, they wanted us to clean their houses and carry their bundles and sleep in their stables. Ask Tata. Tata will tell you about the wife of the commander at Fort San Cristóbal who came here half a century ago and rounded up servants for her house on Sol Street. Rounded them up like cattle and took them off in her military car. We never saw them again.

It wasn't easy for the ones who stayed behind. The sugar land was poor. The seawalls were crumbling. The hurricanes were bad. And there was no money. When I grew up, we saw five cars a day around here—a few públicos, the postman, some administrators from Canóvanas. Hardly enough to notice. But we had our maíz, our yuca. The bay was full of mero, the mangrove swamps full of jueyes. We were happy. Happier than now when the cars go by all day like cockroaches and everybody has government money in their pockets.

I wanted to be a carpenter. That was my dream. I learned the woods—caoba, cedro, roble, pino. Understood each one—the grain, the cut, the strength. The first good thing I learned in school was how to square a piece of wood. I was ten years old. I can still feel the cedar under my hand. My teacher had a big sign over his desk that said, "If you have nothing to do, don't do it here."

Jaime Fernando had a dream too. That's why we became friends. Baloncesto. The Americans think they invented basketball, but it's really a Spanish game. We know more about it, you see. How to put a spell on the ball so it never leaves your hand. How to jump up under the basket and hold your breath so you hang in the air for a minute. Jaime Fernando was the greatest of all the baloncesteros of the village. The greatest in the history of the game. One year his team won twenty-three victories in a row, including the victory against the boys of Toa Baja. I'll never forget the night they came back from that game, very late, the cars circling the village plaza, the boys banging on the sides and shouting, "Chirijí, chirijá, chirijá-já-já, Loiza Indians, rah rah rah!" Everybody woke up and ran down to welcome them—the girls, the old women, the fishermen, the bar-owners. They had heard the cry that said their sons were home, victorious again. Oh, I'd like to be there again, to see the team coming home and hear the chirijí one more time. I would.

Jaime Fernando was small and fast. You saw a coppery blur when he moved down the court. But when he was still you saw a grifo with shining eyes and delicate features and a smile like a flash of white foam. And sweet! If you squeezed him you'd get guarapo juice, the way you get it out of sugar cane.

It ran down his chin in a smile, a gentle word. Lindo—he was always Lindo. Handsome. No one ever called him anything else as long as he lived in this village.

We were friends by the time we were twelve. Panas. You know what panas are? Breadfruit clusters, side by side, high in the shiny green trees. No one could be my pana except Lindo. We made plans. He would play basketball on television and make the Indians as famous as the Globetrotters. He would go on TV, he would meet the president, he would go to Russia. Afterwards, the Americans would give him a parade down Broadway and a million dollars, like they gave Muhammad Ali.

And I would build a tower, a tower of magic ceiba wood, up in the mountains where the clouds touch the ground and the giant ferns grow. And when we were in our magic tower, nothing bad could happen to us. We wouldn't get old and ugly. We wouldn't be too poor to buy a coke or a beer. We wouldn't be chased off the green at the country club because we were the wrong color.

I don't remember the first time we touched each other. I know it was never fooling around. I would fool around with the other boys but not with Lindo. It was always serious. We used to take the ferry across the river to Piñones. We had our own secret place, a beach with sand as fine as sugar, hidden by a forest of sea grape. That was where I kissed him for the first time. I was scared, of course, afraid he wouldn't like it, that he would tell somebody. But it was fine from the first moment. His lips were dark and velvety and I could feel his eyes shining behind his closed lids. Kissing Lindo was like kissing the night.

We didn't do much at first, just looked at each other, compared ourselves the way boys do, then giggled. I don't know what made me take him in my mouth the first time, but it seemed very easy and natural—as natural as shaping wood or playing basketball. He lay back and watched me, his eyes big as moons, while I tasted it and tickled it with my tongue. It made us both feel good, but when he was ready to squirt, I pointed him away from me. We didn't say much going home. We were both wondering what would happen next. I remember how the waves had come up and washed away Lindo's squirt.

It was soon after that I began making santos. Don Nacho, the finest woodcarver on the island, lived down the beach, near Medianía, and when I showed him some of my heads, he took an interest in me. He still carved the little saint figures out of cedar and mahogany—tough woods that resist you with all their strength—instead of the soft woods, yagrumo and pine, that some of the younger santeros use, to step up production. I went over most afternoons after school, while Lindo was practicing on the court, and learned how to use the knives, the glues, the paints in pale and opaque colors. After a year or so, Don Nacho told me I could put my santos next to his on the shipments going to San Juan. My Santiagos, he said, were the best being made.

Did you know that if you get wet in the first rain of May you will stay young forever? One morning when we were sixteen, we heard the rain drumming far out on the ocean. As soon as I heard it, I got up and ran to Lindo's house. He was waiting of course, just as excited as I was. I called and he came out in his yellow satin basketball shorts with the Indian feathers. We ran down the beach as the rain started, and when the drops got heavy, we took off all our clothes. "Look," Lindo cried, whirling down the beach, head thrown back, swallowing the storm.

"Keep us young, Luisa!" I called to the sky. And then we sang the song of the great witch Luisa, for whom this town is named. "That black woman is a witch, a witch," we laughed and screamed, dancing down the beach. And then we asked her to show us the special respect owing to twins, magic twins, and laughed some more.

We were almost to Medianía when the rain stopped. We stopped too, drying off in the sun that had just come out.

There was no one around, no one crazy enough to go dancing down the beach in the rain. And I saw Lindo looking at me in his special way—the full-moon look—and I knew what he wanted. Knew it even though he would never say the words.

I took his wrist and walked him back, away from the shore, to a huge frangipani tree. Under it, we scraped a spot to dry sand and lay down. I moved quickly, turning him face down, forcing his legs apart with my knees. He took me with one brief gasp, and then we were one, rocking back and forth while he cried out, "Give me, give me," and the convulsion shook me just a moment before it shook him. And I knew that Lindo's ass was the sign that I owned him now, just as he owned me. It meant we could trust each other. It was like making a gift, the way Melchior, the black king, made a gift to the Cristo. It didn't matter, all those jokes about men who act like women with other men. We didn't lose respect. And I knew my time would come—the time when I would make the gift like Melchior.

We went in the ocean and washed, quiet at first, then giggling and splashing. Some kids heard us and came out, then joined in. Two boys about eleven or twelve. Watching them, I remembered how it had been when I first met Lindo. Even then I had known everything that would happen. I didn't need a witch or an adivinadora to read it in the cards. I could read it myself—in my hands, my face, my heart.

I began to work for Johnny Vasquez soon after that. Johnny builds concrete boxes—urbanizaciones. They're ant-colonies for human beings. It wasn't carpentry, but it paid. I still worked on my saints, especially Santiago Apóstol, so I wasn't losing skill. Don Nacho told me one day I would take over for him, and become one of the island masters. But whenever he told me that, he was extra critical about my work, so I figured it would be a long time before I would take his place.

About that time, Lindo started working at the Berwynd, odd jobs, sometimes carrying the golf sticks (they let you on the green if you didn't try to play). He talked about basketball, about turning pro, but he didn't know how to do it. There was no place to start. Gradually he started talking less about it. He was getting restless. Bad-tempered too, sometimes. I had my santos but he had—what? A perishing dream. He was starting to change.

So was I. It's hard to explain. But sometimes, after we made love, I would hear strange sounds. Rustlings, crinklings, snappings. Like something growing. And the smell. After we finished I would get the smell of deep earth and rotting flowers and damp. I tried to tell Lindo about it but he laughed in an ugly way and said we needed to bathe ourselves. He'd jump and go in the water, but I'd stay on the sand, under the sea grape, watching his body take on the shine of the water as if he'd been sprayed with glass, noticing the delicate scoring of his chest as he rubbed at the muscles under the coppery skin. At the same time, the smell would grow stronger, as if I were becoming part of the decayed palm trees, the broken coconuts, the crushed blossoms, all around. At last he would call, "Hey negrito, what are you waiting for?" and I'd pull myself up by my roots and drag down to the water. I never wanted to wash. He usually had to pull me in.

We might have gone on like that for a long time if Bernardo hadn't arrived. Lindo was very restless by then, hating his job at the country club, hating the village. Even when we were alone I could feel the anger behind his chest. And now he made me turn over for him. I didn't mind it until I felt him careless about hurting me, eager to pay back his bosses by contempt for my gift—and then I'd make him stop. But still, there were times when the old sweetness came back, when the sugar squeezed out of him, and everything was good again.

Bernardo changed all that.

He took a house just off the highway, a concrete box like all the others there, except that its grillwork was shaped in a spider web. Bernardo was big, over three hundred pounds, white like lightning, and he couldn't see without his glasses. He noticed Lindo right away. I was there when it happened—

Bernardo's big car slamming to a stop on the highway, the door on the passenger side opening, Bernardo motioning us to get in.

"Where you going?" he asked, all smiles. He didn't look at me. He stepped on the gas before Lindo could answer and drove us to his house. "I want to show you where I live," he said, then added, "My house is your house."

We got out because it's bad luck to refuse hospitality like that, but I didn't like it. Bernardo kept close behind Lindo, telling him to turn on the stereo, put on the earphones, look at the color TV—things like that. I don't know where Bernardo got his money. I heard later he worked for the Departamento de Hacienda in San Juan. I figure he learned how to steal the people's money in a big way. Lindo liked all the attention. He liked the machines too. Right away I saw his eyes go full-moon.

Pretty soon Lindo was spending a lot of time at Bernardo's house. He didn't have time to see me. He wouldn't go to our secret beaches. Bernardo said he could get him a Honda.

Everybody knew that Bernardo was paying the boys. They'd collect around his house at night, waiting for an invitation. And some nights Bernardo's friends from San Juan would show up and there'd be a party—eight or ten boys, looking for a chance to steal something. One night two Franciscans from the Cathedral showed up. Bernardo found boys for them too. The priests were scared to death their cardinal was going to find out.

Lindo didn't mind any of this. Bernardo kept him happy with promises. He was going to introduce Lindo to a promoter from the Knicks. He was going to put him in an exhibition game on TV. That Honda was going to show up any day.

Once in a while, when we were alone, Lindo would tell me that he knew Bernardo's promises were all bullshit. But still he went over. He said Bernardo never wanted to touch him—but I wasn't sure whether to believe him.

One day, Lindo and Bernardo went off to San Juan and

didn't come back for three days. I almost went crazy wondering what they were doing, where they were sleeping. Lindo turned up in new clothes—a shirt with stars and moons on it and fancy pants—and a new expression on his face. It was private and secret, like he'd just discovered pirate treasure. He was feeling a little apologetic, so he offered to drive me to our favorite beach. I sat behind him on his Honda, which had just arrived.

We were watching the pelicans dive for sardines when he told me what had happened. They stayed with Bernardo's aunt in Río Piedras, and went to the bars in the Condado at night. There was one they liked the most. Men, mostly gringos, danced with each other. After a while, they went into a dark room behind the bar. When they came out, they were wiping their lips and smiling.

"It's dark as night in there," Lindo said, lying back on the sand. "You can't see a thing."

"Why do they want to do it in the dark?" I looked at him, with his skin like burnt butter and his sinewy arms and legs. "Why wouldn't they want to see you?"

Lindo shrugged. "That's the way they do it."

One of the gringos had liked him a lot, a tall man with gold hair and blue eyes. They had danced. Then they'd gone in the back room, where the man had hugged him, then kneeled down in front of him. Afterward they had gone back to the front, not speaking any more.

Lindo's tight chest rose and fell as he told me this, his long fingers tracing circles in the sand. "Bernardo wants to take me to the States," he said.

I sat up straight. "You want to run away and be an American? An American maricón?"

His face turned hard and nasty. "I'm not going to be a maricón," he hissed. "That's what you are. I can have your ass any time I want it."

For a minute I thought I was going to kill him right there on the beach, under the sea grape. Then I thought, this is Lindo, my pana. If he insults me it doesn't matter.

"My ass doesn't belong to you," I said, but the words sounded empty, insincere. I didn't know what was happening.

He laughed and stood up. We drove back on the Honda and he dropped me at my house and sped off without saying goodbye or looking back.

My mother heard me groaning that night, then she went out. She was making new clothes for the saint and didn't want to work in an unhappy house. After a while I got up and went over to Trinidad's house and bought a black candle. Right away I felt better. Going down to the beach I felt better still. I had a weapon of my own. Not a trip to San Juan or a Honda or an airplane ticket to New York—something else. Something old and secret and more powerful.

I found a wide board with some rusty nails, and sat the candle on a nail. Then I took one of the little launches in front of Pedro Arroyo's house and rowed myself out to the reef. I set the board in the water and whistled three times toward the east, the way Trinidad showed me. Then I lit my candle and called out Bernardo's family name.

I kept the boat near the board, watching it bob around for a long time. The sea was calm and I was afraid the wave might not come, the wave that would extinguish Bernardo's light. But it did at last—a crosswave from the east, under the trade wind—and the candle tipped over. I whispered his name one more time, then rowed back to shore.

Next morning I told my mother I was going to dress up as a woman for the fiesta, a mujer loca in a long dress with a handkerchief around my head. I don't know why I decided to do that. I woke up feeling like something was happening in my room, something new and strong. At first I thought I was going crazy, because of Lindo and Bernardo, but then I decided it wasn't them—it was me. I was changing.

I took one of my mother's dresses and ripped it down the back and sewed some bright striped cloth in for extra width. Then I asked Tata for some of her old skirts and added those to the bottom. When I got through I had a crazy woman—

the craziest you ever saw. I sewed some plastic cherries into a crown of cloth for my head, to top it off.

We started the fiesta at the beach as usual, where the old lady saw the saint coming in on a wave for the very first time. I felt good in my long dress, surrounded by boys and girls with big eyes, watching to see what I would do. I made a few runs at them, pretending to sweep them away with my broom, and they ran away, terrified. The older people kept a respectful distance away from me. Maybe they were afraid. I heard one mother crooning the old song to her child, "That woman is a witch, look at her eyes through a piece of paper," but the child got so frightened he ran away too.

When we marched into the plaza, behind the caballeros and the vejigantes, everybody started screaming. But they screamed at me the loudest, at me, José Antonio, because they had never seen a crazy women so big and powerful before. My tits looked like basketballs and my voice could be heard all across the plaza. I ran around, back and forth, making people pay me, knocking them down if they wouldn't. I saw Lindo and Bernardo under the flamboyán, but I stayed away from them.

The miracle happened on my third time across the plaza. Half the people were drunk then and nobody was paying attention to the fireworks. I don't know where they got those big rockets, but a couple of fires had started in the thatches of the bohíos. One hut had burned to the ground.

But this rocket was the biggest, white and fat like a giant cigar. The men who set it up were drunk, wobbling around and drinking more rum while they held the fire stick. After they lit it, the rocket spluttered on the ground, then climbed slowly up, as high as the roof of Tico's Bar. It hung there for a minute, trembling, then it turned around and headed toward the end of the plaza. I saw Lindo and Bernardo look up, wondering which way to run, and I knew somebody was going to be hurt.

All of a sudden I heard myself shouting, "Santiago, lift up your sword!" The crowd went still and the rocket suddenly died, just like that, and dropped to the ground. A moan went through the crowd and everybody crossed themselves. Some people kneeled down. And everybody looked at me. "A miracle," someone shouted and everybody took up the cry. "A miracle!" A few people came over and touched me, then two girls, virgins fresh like dew, kneeled in front of me and asked for the blessing. I touched their heads and asked God to bless them. And then I understood. The saint had been waiting for me all these years. The beautiful saint had been waiting all these years.

The parties went on all day and night. I stayed in my dress, out of respect, and had a good time dancing and betting on the prizefights and giving blessings. Even Lindo came over, smiling in a grudging way, and told me I had saved his life.

I looked at him, at his sharp delicate face, at his chest as wide and straight as a pine board, and wondered how I could have been angry at him. It seemed like nothing had happened, no time had gone by and we were still young boys filled with dreams. And then Bernardo turned up, red in the face like a baby that's been sucking on a tit too long. He congratulated me for the miracle. I turned and walked away. Trinidad had told me the curse wouldn't work if I talked to the one accursed.

Later I saw him walking around giving money to some of the handsome young men. I knew what he was doing. He was telling them to come by his house later. He was going to have a private party. His friends from San Juan were here. I had seen the Franciscans, white and loose-fleshed inside their brown sacks, licking their lips over the feast to come.

I wondered if I had interfered with Bernardo's destiny by asking the saint to stop the rocket. I was walking home when this occurred to me, and I stopped under a Queen María tree and pulled some of the purple blossoms over me. Maybe the saint was going to punish Bernardo, and I had stopped him. Was it possible that I had missed my chance? I decided I would ask Trinidad about it in the morning.

I didn't have to bother. In the morning Bernardo was dead. It wasn't long before everybody knew what had happened.

He had entertained the boys all night long, one after the other, working overtime. His friends from San Juan had done the same. Finally, very late, everybody had enough. They drove back to the city and Bernardo went to bed. But first they chased the last of the boys away.

One of those last ones was Papo. Mean, with a small head and purple grape eyes, thin shoulders, chicken legs. A half hour later, Papo came back with a gun in his pocket. He banged on the bedroom window. Bernardo got up and Papo showed Bernardo what he had in his pants—and I don't mean the gun. Bernardo was sleepy and said no, but Papo insisted. So Bernardo told Papo to stick it through the iron grill. Papo watched Bernardo's fat lips swallow him up. When it was finished, he asked for money. I don't know what got into Bernardo—maybe he was feeling mean, or didn't hear right. Maybe he figured he'd done enough. Anyway, he told Papo don't bother him about money and started to close the shutter. Papo blinked his purple grape eyes, took out his pistol and shot Bernardo between the eyes. Bernardo fell back on his bed and Papo ran like hell. The judge gave him a year's probation because he said Bernardo had been corrupting the young men of the village.

It was my fault, I knew that. Trinidad knew it too, but she didn't say anything, just looked at me with her hard white eyes like cooked eggs, and mumbled something—maybe a spell to protect her against me. Maybe some other people understood, because they began to treat me differently, keeping a distance, smiling and nodding too much. About that time a man from a hotel in the Condado turned up and asked me to carve saints for his gift shop. He would pay me double what I was getting through Don Nacho. I told him I would only carve my saint, Santiago Apóstol. That was okay with him. So I built the workshop. A place were I could work ten or twelve hours a day with nobody to watch. A place where I could forget Bernardo and the curse and pretend I was just another carver, a santero, and not a man crushed by the power of magic.

Lindo was lost after Bernardo died. He rode his Honda up and down the beach road, over to Río Grande, sometimes as far as Fajardo or Humacao. He had that vacant look you see on addicts or men whose work has been taken away. He stopped going to the Berwynd—said the golfers didn't treat him with respect. Sometimes he asked me for money for gasoline.

I don't know how he found out about the curse. Maybe he saw the black candle when it washed up on the beach. Maybe Trinidad gave him a hint. But one afternoon, late, when I was boiling my glue, he came to the workshop. I stirred while he talked.

"Everybody says you're turning into a witch."

I laughed. "That's just superstition."

"It's that time with the rocket. Why did you do that?"

"I was afraid that if somebody was hurt they would blame the saint. Then it might be the end of the fiesta. The government would close it down."

He shook his head. "Something's happening to you." He waited while I tested the glue. "You put a curse on Bernardo."

I looked up sharply. "Who said that?"

He just laughed, then narrowed his eyes. "Don't try no magic on me," he said. "It won't work because I don't believe in that shit."

I started to tell him that we had always had magic. Being panas was magic. Dancing in the rain and calling on Luisa was magic. Making love under the sea grape was magic. But I didn't.

He told me he was going to New York. Bernardo had already paid for the ticket, and he was going to use it. He looked at me as though he were daring me to stop him.

Something went dark in me when I heard him. I looked at my hands on the wooden handle—claws the color of mahogany. What could they do?

"If you want to go to New York, nobody can stop you, not me, not even the saint," I murmured.

He laughed again, then cursed. I watched him leave, his body straight and stiff, all right angles. He raced the Honda motor in contempt, then roared off. By the time I stopped thinking, the glue had boiled away and I had to start over again.

I didn't see him again until the night of the goodbye party. Somebody said he had gone to one of the other islands, but I had the feeling he had gone to San Juan. Back to the bar where the gringos with ice-blue eyes and golden hair were waiting. Maybe it was a new kind of practice—practicing for life up north.

The boys from the basketball team gave him a wool scarf, probably got it from somebody returned from the States for good. His sister and her friends gave him a guitar made in Spain. He bent over it, his fingers strumming in a golden blur. I gave him a carving of the boy saint, the Santiaguito, the saint looking like Lindo used to look, and the horse standing very high. He turned it around and around, as if looking for something he had lost, and then he smiled at me—a flash of white foam—and I had to look away to keep from remembering too much.

Everybody had a good time. Some of the girls said they were going to run away to New York with him, but they were joking. We danced a bomba, even though it wasn't the season yet, everyone clapping and shouting, taking turns with the riddles. When my turn came, a new poem came to my lips, and everyone looked at me strangely.

> Virgin of Montserrat,
> Virgin of Montserrat,
> Tell me who made your skin so black.

I don't know where the words came from, but in a minute everyone started clapping again and forgot.

I waited so I could be last to say goodbye. We shook hands and then I gave him a hug. I could feel his body go soft and warm, as if he wanted to make one last gift to me—and then it was a pine board again and I let go. It was all over now. The next day I watched the planes as they passed over our bay, wondering which silver bird carried Lindo. I sat on the beach until sunset, then worked all night. By the time the moon went down I had a new image—the black virgin of Montserrat. By the end of the week I had five of them. Later I heard that the tourists in San Juan liked them a lot.

Time went by, today and tomorrow, today and tomorrow. The village seemed very quiet, the old people sitting on their porch steps with fans, the young people making deals with piles of food stamps. Business was good for me. The Turismo people wrote me down in one of their little books and strangers began to turn up, rich people, looking for the famous woodcarver. I always charged them double, since they came so far.

Lindo had been gone six months when his mother got sick. At first we thought it was just a fever, but in a few days it got worse and they called the doctor from Canóvanas. He gave her some injections and told people to stay away from her house.

I went to the Post Office and called my cousin in New York—the daughter of my father's sister. I gave her Lindo's address. A few weeks later she wrote that they couldn't find him. He'd moved and left no address.

By that time his mother was very bad, her face gray, her body shriveled. Her friends took turns sitting with her, in spite of the doctor's order. I knew she was going to die from the typhoid. Nothing could save her. Not the doctors, not the baths of flower water and herbs that Trinidad gave her, not my prayers to the saint.

One night Trinidad came to my workshop and told me

Doña Feliz wanted to see me. I don't know what made me take out my crazy woman costume. It seemed the right thing to do. If I was going to ask for a miracle, it had to be in those clothes, in the bright striped cloth and the plastic cherries. They were my passport to the spirit world—the spirits of water and the spirits of air. Everybody made way for me, backing off and making a line on either side, as I progressed under the palm trees to Lindo's house. They knew my business. They knew my power.

Doña Feliz was sitting up in the back room, the kerosene lamp smoking too much. I blew it out so we sat in the dark, striped by moonlight. I took her hand—it was light as a flower on a cup-of-gold tree. "Where is Lindo?" she whispered, "where is my son?'

"He is here," I answered, knowing it was true.

She leaned back at that, and sighed, "I want to give him my blessing."

I kneeled in front of her, so big and clumsy in my dress, and bowed my head. Her hands rested on my hair like butterflies while she whispered the words. I felt them take root in me, the seeds sprouting, filling the air with fragrance. And then I called on the saint, just like before. "Santiago," I said aloud in the dark room, "lift up your sword." Silence, except for her breathing. A great weariness passed through me. "Santiago, lift up your sword," I repeated, the words heavy. A third time—and then I heard her breathing get shorter, sharper, and I knew the saint hadn't heard.

The door opened and Trinidad came in with another lamp. I could see that Doña Feliz was exhausted. Just before I left, she mumbled something about taking earth from her grave, but I had already thought of that.

I went home thinking of Lindo. That was why she had gotten sick. He was her last son, the youngest. The others were in Detroit, Chicago, Philadelphia. He was the one who had promised to stay, and he had gone away too.

I took off my dress and dropped it in a corner of my workshop. Why had the saint failed me? And then, looking at the rows of figures, I knew. I hadn't done enough. I hadn't taken the responsibility.

The funeral took place on a cool day in January, the palm trees singing under the wind. When the coffin was lowered and everyone picked up a handful of earth to throw on it, I did the same—then turned away. Several people noticed that I slid the earth in my pocket, but said nothing. I walked home slowly, the earth warm against my thigh, wishing things were different. I transferred the dirt to a wooden box I had made the night before. Then I put the box in my suitcase, which was already packed. When I got to New York, the earth from the grave would still be fresh. Doña Feliz would be with me.

On the highway the next morning, waiting for the público to take me to the airport, I knew that only bad things would come from all this. In spite of all the love around him, Lindo would turn it to destruction and hate. But there was no way to change it, no way to stop.

New York looked so frightening from the plane window I didn't want to watch. The woman next to me crossed herself, then kissed her hand as the plane came down. But I didn't need to do that. I was under the protection of the saint from the minute I left home. Still, I didn't want to look at the tall buildings.

My cousin lived in the Bronx, and she met me with her family—two boys I had never seen and her husband, who had been born in Caguas and had dreamed of being a boxer. He worked in a hospital now, in charge of the people who kept it clean. He looked gray in the face, as if all the dust he had swept had gotten stuck there.

I knew it would take a while to find Lindo, so I wasn't in a hurry. I helped my cousin with the house, taking care of the boys, teaching them the games they would never learn in Manhattan—The Three Captives, The Count's Son, Rice with Milk. It was hard to leave the barrio, but one day I took the subway to Times Square and after that it was easier.

Sometimes at night I took out the wooden box with the dirt from Doña Feliz' grave and held it in my hand, not opening it, not letting the spirit escape. I always felt better afterward, better able to accept the terrible cold that penetrates your clothes, accept the people who look at you without seeing, accept the signs and lights and talk of money. The New York people always walk in a straight line—if you don't step out of their way they walk right into you, still talking about money, and after that they stab you with their eyes. Most of the time I felt dark and invisible.

I made myself go down to the streets with smaller numbers, after I had been in Times Square. I walked around the streets and the river, the buildings sticking into it like rotten fingers, the garbage floating everywhere. I saw the gringos Lindo had told me about, the gringos Bernardo had entertained on the feast-days—but I didn't see Lindo.

One night I went into one of the bars near the river. It was filled with pale men in uniforms, gleaming in leather and steel. They looked like a race of savages—silver savages. No one spoke to me and the bartender pretended not to hear when I asked for a beer. After a while I left. None of these men would have told me where Lindo was, even if I knew how to ask.

That night, I sat with the box of dirt in my hand for a long time, wondering if the time had come to open it. I was very sad, sadder than I had been since the day we met Bernardo and he began to show Lindo all his machines. I even thought about giving up and going home. Lindo was lost. Even if I could find him, he would be lost.

And then, suddenly, the box of dirt moved in my hand. Not much, just a little jump, as if the earth had turned over, or had risen and was knocking on the lid. "What is it?" I asked, my heart pounding, "What is it, Doña Feliz?" There was no answer, of course, and the box didn't move again. But I had my answer.

The next day I went to the colmado and bought olives, cheese, fruits and a white tablecloth. I asked my cousin and her husband to be ready at nine o'clock, after the boys were asleep. They would have to help me, if there was trouble. I rested all day, trying to keep myself calm.

Just before nine, I put the white tablecloth on the table in the kitchen, and spread out the food for Doña Feliz' spirit. Then I went and put on my crazy woman clothes, to signify that I was ready. After that I poured flower water on my hands and face. When all that was done, I took the box and put it in the center of the table, with the olives, cheese and fruit.

We sat for a while, holding hands, waiting. Then I got up and found a record of the Ave Maria and put it on the phonograph. The spirit possessed me on the way back to the kitchen. "Good evening," said Doña Feliz, in a sweet voice. I began to shake, and extended my arms. Then I began to have trouble breathing.

They helped me to the couch. I was trembling so much they had to hold me down. Then I heard Doña Feliz whispering in my ear, and the trembling stopped. I felt myself getting calmer as I listened. Finally, I crossed my arms over my chest and moved into the spirit world.

Doña Feliz was wearing her white dress, the dress she always wore when she marched with Santiago of the Women on the second feast-day. She carried a bouquet of white carnations in one arm and in the other a photograph of Lindo in his basketball uniform. She stopped when she saw me and held up the picture. "Now we will find my son," she said in a gentle voice. After that she smiled and said, "I will go with you, I will do whatever you want." I stirred at this, a pain sharp in my chest. "I can't find him, Doña Feliz, I don't know where to look." But she smiled sweetly again and shook her head. Just before she disappeared she held up the picture again.

I woke up feeling refreshed. The room was thick with earth smells and flowers. Even my cousins noticed it.

That night I dreamed about the bar where they refused

to serve me and I understood that next time Lindo would be there. Doña Feliz had sent the dream.

I waited three days before going back. Then, late one night, I took the subway. It was a long walk to the river. I joined a stream of men walking in the same direction. They didn't notice me. Perhaps I had merged with the night. Perhaps Doña Feliz had made me invisible. Perhaps I was still in my dream. But I followed them, the men shining like the silver plankton of La Parguera, to the door of the bar. At first I thought the man at the door, who was all covered with bright tattoos, wouldn't let me in. Then he changed his mind and motioned me to enter.

I stood for a long time, not moving. The place was full. I saw cowboys and paratroopers. Soldiers and generals. Prisoners and guards. I saw whips and handcuffs and boots and chains. But most of all I saw pride, a cold, cold pride.

I did not see Lindo.

The bartender let me buy a beer but forgot to give me change. I waited for a long time, but finally moved away with the crowd. They seemed to be drifting to another room. I let myself be carried along.

It was very dark inside there and I could hardly see. Gradually I became aware of certain things—a huge skull with an electric light inside. Some little folding beds. A bathtub. Toilets, open for everyone to see. Strong odors, sounds. Filth. Excrement.

Was it possible that Lindo would come to a place like this?

Suddenly the men around me got excited, heaving and moaning as if someone with a huge spoon had stirred them up. They moved and I glimpsed a man writhing on the floor, held down by the boots of two policemen. One of the boots dug into his groin. Then the crowd shifted and I couldn't see any more.

I drifted over to one of the bathtubs. There was a man sitting in it, shining with sweat. Over him another man squatted, balancing himself on the rim of the tub. I didn't want to watch, didn't want to hear, didn't want to believe—it was too cruel, too strange. But I stayed, watching, as the man in the tub opened his mouth and swallowed.

The crowd got more excited, pulling at each other while a low hum as of a thousand insects rose from their throats. They seemed to merge, to melt into a huge swarm of whiteness—the whiteness of tombs and moonlight, of snow and ice. The human race has died, I thought, and a race of ghosts has taken their place.

And then, on a raised platform at the end of the room, I saw what I had never thought to see in this life. A man, slender and beautiful, was shackled to a board, his arms outspread, his legs chained together. Someone went up and put something to his nose and his body jerked. My heart stopped and my breath went cold. Was this what the black Virgin of Montserrat had seen on the worst day of her life? Then I got dizzy and went to the wall, looking for a place to sit down.

It was there, against the wall, that I saw him. It took me a moment because he looked so different. His face was drawn and old. His chest and arms were thin and bare. But there was something else too. It took me another moment to understand. He was white. As white as the ghosts around us. Some evil spirit had bleached his skin, faded his flesh, and he had become ... what?

I stared at him, knowing it must be a trick of the light or the dark. The same Lindo was inside that snowy skin, the Lindo I knew. I got up and went over to him, putting out my hand to touch him. But then I drew back, afraid of being burned by that pale fire.

"What are you doing here?" he said.

That was all. No greeting, no hug, not even a handshake.

"I came to look for you. I promised your mother."

His eyes came to life at that. "Mamá?"

"Yes. She wanted me to ... tell you something."

He came closer. "What?"

I looked around at the insect swarm. "I can't tell you here. You have to come outside."

He looked at me as if he didn't believe me and I waited, knowing the spirit would help me.

"Now?"

"Yes. Now."

I turned and fought my way to the outer room, Lindo behind me. I thought I saw a movement behind him, following, but I wasn't sure. When I reached the street I took a deep breath. My lungs hurt from the air of the cave. I leaned against a car and waited.

He came out, looking left and right. I could see that my impression of whiteness was not correct, or only partly correct. He had faded, but there were still flashes of copper, glints of gold. I wondered how much longer it would be before he was completely white.

"What did mamá say?" he asked quickly. Then he looked over his shoulder.

The door opened before I could answer. I felt him cringe slightly.

"Quick," he said.

"She wants you to come home. Back to the island."

He shook his head. "I can't."

"Why?"

He didn't answer and a shudder, light as a breeze, rippled through him. A figure had stepped into the lamplight of that infernal street and I could see that he had some deadly connection to Lindo.

"Why not?" I asked again, but he didn't answer.

The man in the doorway was barechested like Lindo, but powerfully built. His shoulders were broad, his arms massive and marbled with veins. And he was completely white, of a whiteness you might have seen on Satan's suit on his wedding day in hell. But worst of all was his face—a death's-head dug up from a continent of ice.

We were both watching him. He ran his heavy hand down his chest, past the buckle of his belt. Slowly, proudly, he began to massage himself. I heard Lindo's breath and felt his spirit waver. I could smell defeat.

"Lindo," I hissed, "come to my cousin's. We can talk."

I don't think he heard me. "Lindo!" I called again, but he had turned away and begun to move toward his friend—or owner. The blue eyes in the death's-head flickered from Lindo to me, calmly. Lindo was already a few paces away, moving with a dead drugged air. The death's-head nodded. "Get inside," he said.

And then I knew what I had to do.

I jumped him from behind, spinning him around and down to the pavement, holding his thin bare body in my dark arms. He was furious, twisting savagely, reaching for my throat while I pushed his head against the pavement. But I had the advantage. I had always been able to beat Lindo in a fight. I beat him when we wrestled on the beach and I beat him when we fought in school. He was faster but I was stronger, and it's strength that wins in the long run.

We turned over and over, cursing and hitting while silver faces peered at us through the bar windows and the death's-head watched. But I knew Lindo couldn't win. Couldn't... possibly. He was fighting to lose his soul while I was fighting to save it. The spirit was on my side.

I had him pinned at last, breathing hard under the dark mountain of my body. His eyes were huge with hatred and he spat in my face.

"Your mother has died," I said. "She died two weeks ago of the typhoid."

I felt him go limp under me.

"Your name was on her lips. She gave me the blessing to pass on. I brought it with me."

His eyes grew round and glittered.

"But not here. Not here. Home."

I moved back on my haunches and let him sit up, aware that the faces at the windows had turned away, bored, now that the fighting was finished. Lindo twisted away, hiding his face.

And then, suddenly, the death's-head was bending over him, helping him up. I said nothing.

Lindo stood silently, his head still turned. His friend pulled at his elbow, pushing him inside. I waited, knowing the spirit would not fail me.

Lindo broke away and came toward me. "I'll go with you," he said.

And then, suddenly, he was hugging me and sobbing and calling on his mother. I had the impression that Doña Feliz was wrapping us both in a benediction. "Lindo," I whispered, rocking him as if he were a baby. "Lindo."

His friend called him once or twice—Jimmy was the name he used—but we didn't pay any attention. We limped up the street, arms around each other, as if we were not in New York, not in that place of shades and shadows, but back at the beach, under the seawind, rooted in each other's bodies, the air around us heavy with fragrance.

At the apartment, I made him kneel down and bend his head. I gave him the blessing, hearing Doña Feliz' voice as I repeated her words. Then I told him about the fever and the doctor and the funeral. He listened quietly. Once or twice he shivered and whispered, "mamá." I showed him the wooden box and how the lid could slide back and forth. "Ceiba wood," I said. "I was going to build our tower out of magic ceiba wood, remember?"

He didn't answer, just took the box and sat quietly, holding the soil from his mother's grave.

After a while he began to talk about his life in New York. It had started out well. He got a job with a health club, cleaning up, but they liked him and promised to make him a trainer before long. One of the owners took an interest in him, invited him to his house, showed him the bars. He took Lindo to a few parties where he left his clothes at the door and swallowed or smoked or sniffed a whole drugstore of plants and medicines.

"Everybody liked me, they said I was beautiful." He smiled. I looked at his thin arms, his whited chest, and thought of the Caribs, another race of savages who had consumed their victims. What would his new friends have said if they had seen him years ago when his skin blended with the sand and reflected the fires of the sun? Did they know how beautiful Lindo could be?

They taught him new things to do, new ways to feel excited. The people here have machines for sex, and Lindo got in the habit of using them. He had moved from one person, one machine, to another. Finally he had met the man who was at the bar with him—that superb creature with the face of death. Mike, Lindo said, was the finest machine of all—tuned like a racing car. There was nothing Mike would not do, or make Lindo do. As he told me about it, his voice grew respectful, and I thought about the gods the Caribs worshiped and how they required victims. But then, when he was telling me the strangest story of all, he stopped and shook his head. "The horror, José," he whispered, "you can't imagine the horror."

"That's finished now," I told him.

He nodded, and I talked about my plan—to open my own shop for selling my saints in San Juan. Lindo would be the manager, in charge of everything, sharing the profits. He liked the idea of being his own boss, of our working together on the island. It would be exciting, I told him, more exciting than the life here in New York. As we talked he took on new color. He flushed and darkened. I could almost see the blood flowing. Pretty soon we were laughing. And I remembered our other plans, the old dreams, and I thought—now they're going to come true.

We slept together in one of the beds. He was nervous about my touching him—maybe he had been touched too much—so I just rested one arm on his shoulder, a bridge from my body to his. I could feel my mind loosen from all the troubles of the past few months. It was all behind us—Bernardo, Doña Feliz, New York.

Just before I fell asleep I heard a noise on the table where I had put the box. I paid no attention. I didn't think the spirit of Doña Feliz might be restless. Wasn't my work finished? Hadn't I kept my promise? Hadn't I passed on the blessing?

Wasn't her son asleep at my side, his eyelids folded like moth's wings over his astonished eyes? Yes, I told myself, feeling Lindo's skin smooth under my hand, yes, yes, yes. I slept like an innocent all night long.

In the morning he was gone.

He had slipped away from my dreams, from my arms, gliding from the bedroom like a ghost, making his way back to the nightmare, to the horror. The machines had claimed him again—perhaps they had never really let go, and all the talk of managing the shop was just something to make me happy, to keep me from seeing the truth.

I jumped out of bed and took up the box of earth. I hurled it against the wall. It broke and brown lumps dribbled onto the floor. It had all been a mistake. There never was any magic. It was a superstition—a trick of the island, the dark people, their lost heritage. I had been playing games in a city where no one played games. I went over and stamped on the brown lumps, thinking I was desecrating Doña Feliz' grave.

I went to the airport later that day. As the plane lifted up and I saw the tall buildings, I swore that I would never see them again. I would never come back. When I got home I burned down my workshop and all my saints. When the fire was high I took my crazy woman dress and tore it into rags and threw it in. It was the last thing I could do.

When you go back to New York you will probably find Lindo in that bar by the river. You will see a little man with silver skin and eyes like dead moons who answers to the name of Jimmy. When you see him, mention my name. Tell him that José Antonio is still here in the village. Tell him José Antonio is still here and has not forgotten.

And now, my friends, it is time to say goodnight.

J OSÉ BOWED HIS HEAD when he had finished and we sat quietly. Nobody moved. Nothing could be heard except the tree frogs pounding their rhythms and the sound of water lapping. At last he muttered something and stood up. We watched him move through the dark toward the front door.

When he opened it, we could see the moon. For a moment he was bathed in its light—a huge man spangled in silver—and then he stepped outside and we could see only a vague mass, formless as the sea, impenetrable as the night. And we understood that he had returned to the darkness from which he came—to his earth, to his home, to his incorruptible dream.

Death in San Juan

BILL HOLTMANN lowered the binoculars and peered at the beach, seven stories down. It was not right. This stretch of Atlantic had been declared unfit for swimming or surfing, yet the Puerto Ricans were wallowing in the waters as if they were distilled from purest springs. Bill raised the binocs again, swiveling them out to sea. There were at least a dozen surfers out there, half-buried in the blue, bobbing up and down like seahorses.

He was about to swing the instrument back to shore when he caught sight of another surfer, much farther out. The boy must be crazy. He was almost at the reef. There were sharks, barracudas. Bill adjusted the focus and found that the boy was actually a man—a man wearing a straw fedora with a narrow brim. Bill drew in his breath reprovingly. The man had a hairline mustache and weathered-looking chest. He was obviously over forty. He was moving his hands in the water in a vague way, as if he had no intention of going anywhere.

Disgusted, Bill swung the binoculars to shore. They were Zeiss, fifteen power. The blurring movement made him dizzy and he lowered them, massaging the skin around his eyes. In a few minutes he would have to go shopping. Tomorrow, with the apartment full of guests, there would be no time. But first, he wanted to take a last look at the sign put up by the Department of Public Health.

He read the Spanish twice, his irritation rising. *La calidad de las aguas en este sector hace las mismas temporalmente no reco-*

mendable para bañarse. Yes, it was forbidden to bathe at this beach because the waters were polluted. It was common knowledge that some of the private homes emptied their wastes into the sea. This had been going on for years. Only recently had the public health people posted the signs. The purpose was to keep the bathers out until the sewage system was corrected. Foolish dream! The ocean was full of splashing, shouting people. Tourists had been doing the same all winter and now that it was June, the summer vacationers were ignoring the signs just as assiduously.

Bill sighed and clapped the lid on the binoculars. The shopping had to be done. Pipo and Migdalia and the rest were arriving tonight. Everything had to be ready.

Bill always came to Puerto Rico in June, opening up his beachfront apartment for the great name-day feast of the capital city—San Juan Bautista. He hadn't missed the *fiesta patronal* in years. And of course the Ramos family, his Puerto Rican friends in New York, always made the same pilgrimage, arriving the day before the holiday eve. They always stayed with him.

Bill stood up and headed toward the kitchen. This year, since the waters at their customary beach were polluted, there would be a problem. He directed his thoughts toward it—he was not the sort to avoid reflecting on distasteful things—and foresaw what would happen. His suggestion that they transfer the party to another beach would be ignored. He would then announce that he did not intend to go in the water with them. There would be shouts, cries of outrage. He would remain firm. He was not going into that polluted sea, not for the Ramos family, not even for St. John the Baptist himself.

But even as he decided this, another impulse asserted itself. Not in his mind—that would have been impossible—but in his chest. His heart had started a rapid, anxious beating. Yes, on the balcony of his apartment overlooking the white strand of beach, the drumbeat in his chest reminded him that his decision not to join the *fiesta* was having unpleasant repercussions.

As he turned into the kitchen, he had a last glimpse of the beach. The waters were deceptively clean-looking. But he had seen the yellowish stream emptying from the rusted pipe. How could he join the Ramos family tomorrow at midnight, when the time came to wade into the sea seven times—*seven times!*—to ensure good luck in the coming year? Yet, how could he refuse to join that circle of love and fellowship? It would be almost as wrong as denying his responsibilities for Guillermo Ramos, who was his godson and had been named after him.

Bill leaned his head against the refrigerator. It was frost-free and taller than he was. There was no help for it. He would have to stay on shore.

Bill did the shopping—the stores were mobbed before the holiday—then took a taxi to another beach, which was untainted. He didn't like the crowd there; they were mostly North Americans. Amazing how they kept their distance from each other, even on a beach. Puerto Ricans were not afraid of physical closeness. He had noticed that about them from the very beginning, when he had arrived from Milwaukee to take up his residency at St. Luke's Hospital in New York.

On his evening strolls up Broadway in those days, Bill had gradually become aware of increasing numbers of dark and exotic-looking people. These newcomers seemed to behave differently from the older residents, who were mostly Irish or Jewish and who stayed indoors a lot. The Puerto Ricans seemed to gather on stoops and corners, laughing and dancing to the Latin rhythms on their portable radios. The women often looked at Bill in an appraising way, which he found refreshing. He was then in his late twenties and attractive. His hair was ash-blond and wavy, his skin rosy, his muscle tone good.

He had also been charmed by the men, especially the older ones with rain-barrel figures. He liked the way their heavy frames conveyed both power and dignity. Their simple, direct manner filled him with confidence.

About six months after Bill first began to notice the Puerto Ricans, he signed up at Berlitz for a course in Spanish. He did this not only because he liked educational projects, but also because the thought of communicating with these febrile people of the streets excited him. He worked hard at Spanish and progressed rapidly. Only in preparing for his specialty boards in radiology had he worked harder. It seemed that once he had the key to the Puerto Ricans' speech, he would find the key to other things he was looking for. He didn't ask himself what these might be, because he was not an introspective sort. It was enough to know that in the neon-spattered wilderness of upper Broadway there were men and women living rich impetuous lives, lives to which speaking their language might give access. They seemed the perfect antidote to the profession he had chosen, which involved reading shadows on a screen all day in search of the spoor of death.

However, Bill was surprised to find that even after several months of study he could not communicate very well. This was made clear when he found himself alone in an elevator with a strange operator. This was the first Puerto Rican to be hired at Bill's hospital, which was in Queens, and Bill found himself uneasy at the prospect of speaking Spanish.

"*Buenos días,*" he remarked slowly and loudly, "*deseo ir al tercer piso.*"

The operator, a hoop-chested man with gold teeth and mahogany skin, looked at him with large puzzled eyes, then barked something that sounded like "*Bweh-dee-toto.*" After that, he took the car to the third floor. As Bill walked down the hall, he repeated the phrase to himself. *Bweh-dee-toto.* What did that mean? The phrase seemed to have nothing to do with the Spanish demonstrated at Berlitz by Señorita Morales.

It wasn't until the next morning, as he was doing his twenty minutes of vocabulary building over coffee, that the words took on meaning. The elevator man had said, "*Buenos días, doctor.*" He had been returning Bill's greeting. Bill then resolved to terminate his lessons at Berlitz when the current course was finished.

But his first real break came a few weeks later when he ran into an employee from the hospital. This occurred at the corner of 110th Street and Broadway. The employee was a young woman recently hired to work in the cafeteria. Bill didn't know her name but when he saw her carrying a bag of groceries, he darted over. "You're from the hospital!" he cried out, too loudly. She was frightened for a moment, then nodded. *"Oh-spee-tahl!"* she replied. *"Sí, sí."*

Bill took the bag of groceries from her and walked her home. She was from Aibonito, a town in the mountains of Puerto Rico, and had arrived in New York only recently. She spoke no English. Her name was Renée Ramos.

Renée lived with her aunt and uncle and their two sons in an old tenement the color of tobacco juice. Bill went upstairs with her. He knew the building, had often observed people on the front stoop, but had never gone inside before. In fact, this was his first visit inside any tenement in the Spanish quarter. As the odor of olive oil reached his nostrils, he felt intensely excited. He seemed to be getting nearer the heart of things. He and Renée had been speaking Spanish. By a miracle, he had understood almost everything she said.

Renée's aunt came out of the kitchen when she heard them. She was a slender nervous woman who enlarged her dark eyes when she saw the visitor. Again, Bill found himself linguistically equal to the occasion. He took her hand warmly in both of his and introduced himself. Her remarks were perfectly understandable.

When he found out that her first name was Migdalia, he began using the honorific, Doña Migdalia. According to his textbooks, this was the respectful form of address for older women. Renée's aunt, who was about forty, appeared surprised the first time she heard herself addressed this way, but as Bill continued to use it she seemed to relax. However, she kept her black eyes fastened on Bill's pink face with something like fascination.

Bill accepted their offer of coffee, and as Doña Migdalia went into the kitchen, he sat in an easy chair and conversed with Renée. Her face was small and heart-shaped, her eyes caramel-colored, her figure on the thin side but nicely made. Bill expressed his pleasure at being in a real Puerto Rican home, but Renée paid little attention to this and told him about her anxieties about life in New York. She was afraid of many things—the subways, the tall buildings, the rudeness of the shopowners. Fortunately just as Bill was losing track of her meaning, her aunt appeared with a tray.

It was then that he had his first vocabulary lesson in Puerto Rican cooking. As he took up each delicacy, he asked the correct name for it. His little notebook was soon filled with words like *bizcocho, pastel, empanada* and *churro*. He wrote each down carefully, his tastebuds trembling with the splendor of the syllables, then resolved to speak to the head dietician at the hospital in the morning. He would suggest that these foods be added to the weekly menu.

He had a hard time getting away. Doña Migdalia wanted him to stay and meet her husband and two sons. Renée, clinging to his arm, whispered, *"Mi casa es su casa,"* which he did not realize was a traditional expression of hospitality. Both women wrapped the remaining sweets for him and urged him to come back soon for a real Puerto Rican meal. As Bill descended the stairs, he was filled with satisfaction. He had been right about the Puerto Ricans. They *were* warm and hospitable, unlike the native New Yorkers. It seemed that he had reached the end, or the beginning, of a long trip. His loneliness in New York, his lack of friends, his visits to the bars and baths for brief, anonymous sex—all these events, so devoid of real satisfaction, could come to an end. He would have a place where he was welcome. A place far more interesting than the one he had left behind in Milwaukee.

A FEW DAYS after his first visit, Bill was asked back for dinner. The invitation was extended with shyness by Renée, from behind the cafeteria counter at the hospital, and

Bill accepted promptly. On the appointed night, he found his heart thumping with pleasure as he climbed the stairs of the tenement. He felt no shyness at the prospect of an evening with strangers, which was unusual. He carried a bottle of Barrilitos rum, which he had been told was the best Puerto Rican brand.

The man who opened the door was thick and round as a rain barrel and his skin was the color of dried oak leaves. He was wearing a short-sleeved white shirt. This man beamed at him, then pumped his hand and rumbled, *"Un honor, un honor."*

Still holding Bill's hand, he ushered him into the living room and introduced him to his two sons as *el doctor.* The younger boy, about ten, was called Junior. The elder was known as Huracán, a nickname he had picked up at the gym where he was training as a boxer. He was about seventeen. The boys shook hands rather diffidently, measuring the stranger with bright glances. The elder Ramos opened the bottle of Barrilitos and poured two drinks. As Bill watched, he had the feeling that this was some kind of Latin ritual. When the glass, half filled with amber liquid, was offered to him, he murmured, *"Salud, pesetas y amor."* He had just come across this expression in a new phrase book. As the sweet liquor tingled down his throat, he felt more at home than he could ever remember.

He was disappointed to find that both Junior and Huracán spoke English quite well. The family had been in New York for several years; only Renée was a recent arrival. But he was also pleased to find that the elder Ramos, whose first name was Filiberto, spoke little English. As they chatted, Bill wondered if he should address his host as Don Filiberto. It was certainly the correct thing to do. On the other hand, everything was so jolly and informal here, using the honorific might create a distance between them. As he downed the rest of his rum, he decided that the need to be correct outweighed everything and he said enthusiastically, *"Cuánto me alegro de estar aquí, Don Filiberto!"*

This had an unexpected effect on his host. He threw back his massive head and roared with laughter, then got up, went over to Bill and pounded him on the back. Finally, when he got his breath, he cried, *"No soy Don Filiberto! Soy Pipo!"*

Bill could hardly believe his ears. The man not only wanted to be his friend, he wanted to be called by his nickname, Pipo. He glanced at the two boys. They were grinning sheepishly. Then he replied, *"Bueno, Pipo, usted tiene que llamarme Bill!"*

"Beel! Okay, Beel," Pipo roared, pounding him some more. *"Panas!"* he cried, louder. *"Somos panas!"*

Bill looked around in confusion. That was a new word.

"Means you and him is buddies," Huracán offered.

"Ah, *panas!*" Bill took out his little notebook and wrote down the word while the others watched in amazed silence. "*Panas* means good friends?" he asked Huracán.

"Yeah, real good friends."

When the entry was finished, he looked at Pipo, who had poured himself another drink. Pipo was staring at him, his eyes dark wells of curiosity. Bill had the feeling that Pipo was trying to find a place for him, but whether in his thoughts or his heart or merely in his home he wasn't sure. Soon after that, the women came in and supper was served.

As Bill tried each dish, he made an entry in his notebook, which he had placed beside him on the table. The family helped him, especially the boys, who knew the English for everything. As the meal progressed, Bill expanded more and more. This was delightful. Suddenly, hardly aware of what he was saying, he sang out, "I'm going to Puerto Rico next month!"

He had made no vacation plans yet, but this seemed the natural thing to say. The news was received with joy. "Puerto Rico!" Renée echoed, swaying her body. "Puerto Rico," Pipo rumbled, tapping his knife against his plate.

Then everyone chimed in with advice on what to see. Best of all, Doña Migdalia insisted that he go to Aibonito to take some gifts to their relatives. Bill listened with pleasure. Not only would he visit the island, he would have entrée to the homes there. As he looked around the table, at the solid figure of Pipo, the virgin sweetness of Renée, the coiled grace of Huracán and Junior, it occurred to him again that he had finally found a place where he belonged. Then he began writing the Puerto Rican addresses in his notebook.

IN THE WEEKS before his departure for the island, Bill spent many evenings with the Ramos family. They settled into a routine. First, the ritual offering of rum (he switched to Don Quijote, which Pipo said was best). Then the meal, which usually included one traditional dish, plus bananas. After dinner, Pipo and Bill played dominoes. Bill hadn't played this since he was a child, but it never bored him because he enjoyed doing it with Pipo. At the climaxes of each game, Pipo would cry out in exaggerated pain or pleasure. At the end, he would fall back gleefully. Bill usually let him win.

But gradually, in these weeks before his trip, he became aware that his interest in the Ramos family was puzzling them. He noticed this first when Doña Migdalia asked if he would like to take Renée to a church dance on Saturday. He declined, saying that he was on duty at the hospital, which was true, but he might have suggested an alternate date. When he didn't, he found her staring at him in a thoughtful way.

About a week later, Bill found himself alone with Migdalia's younger sister, Teresita, a divorced woman in her early thirties. Teresita was fine-boned, with features of extraordinary delicacy. She had always given him a full, unabashed stare when they crossed paths, but this time she went further. Alone after dinner (the others had unexpectedly found errands in the neighborhood), Bill was invited to sit beside her on the couch. Suddenly Teresita put her hand over his and placed both between the soft mounds of her breasts. *"Tengo un fuego en mi corazón,"* she whispered. Bill jerked his hand back, as if the fire in her heart had singed him, whereupon she fixed him with a look of dawning contempt. They spent the rest of the time making small talk—he eagerly, she with a boredom she made no effort to hide. When the others returned, she walked out with an angry toss of her head.

The next solo event took place at Huracán's gym. He had invited Bill to watch him work out, so one afternoon Bill made the trip to a decayed brick building and pushed a bell that said Cucu Perez, Boxing Champ. Upstairs he found Huracán working a light bag in the corner. Bill had to admit that the young man's form was excellent. He tapped the bag until it beat a steady rhythm against the ceiling, his tightly muscled arms blurring with the rapid movements.

After Huracán had worked out for a few minutes, he stopped and smiled at Bill. As he did so, he smoothed the front of his shorts with the vast thumb of his glove—once, twice, three times. Bill shifted uneasily, turning to look around. They were alone. He recalled the solitary hour with Teresita. Huracán returned to the bag and began to hit it in a desultory way, stopping from time to time to look at Bill. At last he said, "Time for a shower, you wanna come?" Bill's first impulse was to say no, but thinking that might sound stand-offish, he agreed. They went to a lavatory at the rear of the building, where Huracán stripped down. The skin under his shorts was lighter than the rest—a gleaming ochre. Huracán stepped into the shower, howling with mock anguish as he adjusted the faucets, then began to soap himself. Bill turned away while he did so and combed his hair in the mirror. But he was forced to turn back when Huracán called his name. He saw, to his consternation, that the young man was soaping his sex organ, now semi-erect, and smiling at him with a mixture of fear and lewdness.

Bill smiled back, quite nervous now, and resumed combing his hair. Then he told Huracán he would wait for him in the coffeeshop downstairs.

Bill didn't call the Ramos family for several weeks after this episode. He even wondered if he should stop seeing them altogether. It was obvious that things had taken a wrong turning. He had never permitted himself to think of them in sexual terms. And now it was clear that the same was not true of them. But in the days when he refrained from calling, keeping busy at the hospital and with his Spanish studies, he experienced an acute sense of loss. New York without the Ramos clan seemed cold and empty. His apartment was boring, his head full of echoes. He found himself spending a lot of time in the back rooms of bars and once in a huge empty warehouse on the river where solitary men stalked each other. He left hurriedly when he realized that he did not really care whether he was mugged or beaten or robbed.

The next day, with great hesitation, Bill called the house. Doña Migdalia answered, and from the concern in her voice, Bill knew that he had been missed. Missed in spite of his disinterest in Renée, his rejection of Teresita, his misunderstanding with Huracán. He had been missed—it came to him in a rush of joy—as a member of the family.

He accepted an invitation to dinner that night. They were going to have *asopao*.

The meal had the character of a reunion. Renée told about her first visit to Coney Island, Huracán told about changing gyms. Pipo warned that the longshoremen were going out on strike. Bill was enthralled by all this. It seemed that he had passed a test of some kind and that now a special place was reserved for him.

After dinner he played dominoes with Pipo, winning easily. Pipo didn't seem to mind. Bill realized he need not lose in order to keep his franchise in the house. He might win every night for a year and Pipo would still enjoy his company.

As he stood in the front hall saying goodnight, Pipo and the boys gave him the traditional *abrazo*. But when he turned to Doña Migdalia, she held out her hand, palm down. Her eyes were shining. Bill instantly knew what she wanted to do, had seen her do it for Huracán and Junior dozens of times—in fact, every time they left the house. She wanted to give him *la bendición,* her blessing. Heart pounding, he bent his head. He felt her lips brush his hair. *"Que Diós te bendiga,"* she whispered. When he straightened up, everyone was smiling at him, and he seemed to be standing in a blaze of light, even though it was ten o'clock at night.

The first trip to the island was a complete success. The Ramos clan was intertwined with many others. Bill was handed from group to group. The word had gone out—he was to be treated like a member of the family. As he sat in various parlors, mostly in simple two-room wooden houses, it occurred to him that there was nothing of Milwaukee left in him. All that had been expunged and another past had taken its place—a past composed of Taino Indians and the songs of Rafael Hernández and dozens of dishes featuring bananas. He was a new Holtmann, forever unknown to the American branch of the family.

As the years went by, Bill knew that his immersion in Puerto Rican culture was a topic of much gossip at the hospital, especially after he became chief of the Radiology Department. The nurses, he knew, thought it strange that he should remain a bachelor, suspecting that he was sexually dysfunctional. Although he paid no attention to all this, there were times, alone in his apartment, when Bill wondered at the strangeness of life. Then he wondered if he had missed something important, had destroyed some chance for deeper happiness, by building his life around the Ramos family and their friends. These thoughts were always accompanied by intense, but fleeting depression, so he tried to avoid them. But in the last year, his depression had become worse, accompanied by sick headaches. At the same time he began to suffer from sudden, unexplained bouts of tachycardia. Only when he was with his Puerto Rican friends, speaking Spanish, was he somewhat content.

THE CROWD AT THE San Juan airport this evening was large. Many people were arriving for the San Juan Bautista celebration. As Bill stood near the gate, straining for a glimpse of the Ramos family, his bad temper of this morning and his worry about the polluted beach were forgotten. There they were! Pipo leading the way, looking a little shrunken in his summer suit—he was 63 now—followed by Migdalia and the rest. Pipo had a dreamy look on his face and even Migdalia, who smiled only rarely since Junior had been killed in Vietnam, was beaming. She was holding her grandson Guillermo, who was also Bill's godson, by the hand. Behind her were Huracán and his wife Patricia. Both families lived near each other in suburban New Jersey now.

As their eyes searched the crowd, looking for him, Bill sensed how much their native soil—*su tierra*—meant to them. Proudly, he understood that he was part of their homecoming too. In fact, he had bought the apartment here mostly for that reason. They cried out when they saw him and hugged him warmly. How familiar their forms felt—fat and thin, soft and muscular, sweet-scented and sour. He carried Guillermo downstairs to the luggage disposal. In the taxi to the apartment, they filled him in on all the latest happenings in their lives.

He didn't broach the subject of the beach pollution until after dinner. As expected, they were skeptical. Pipo, who always sat at the head of the table here, expressed his disdain by calling Bill *doctor*. Huracán thought the idea of staying away was absurd. "Everybody's gonna be on the beach tomorrow night," he said, playing an imaginary bongo on the tabletop, "why should we stay home?"

"We don't have to stay home," Bill said, "we just don't go in the water."

"That's bad luck," Huracán affirmed. "I told the guys at work I'm gonna bring us another good year. I gotta go in for that." He worked as the manager of a used car firm now, where he was known as Ralph. Three nights a week he attended Rutgers, where he was studying for a degree in business administration.

"You can have a good year without going in the water," Bill replied, "it's just a superstition."

"We haven't missed in five years, and they turned out good, right *papá?*" He repeated the statement in Spanish. Pipo nodded sagely.

Repressing his irritation, Bill went into the kitchen. He decided to make a last appeal.

Migdalia listened but it was clear she was not impressed. She told him that all her friends had been bathing at this beach since the signs went up and no one had gotten sick. Then she said the signs must have been put up by the communists to scare away the tourists. After this, Bill gave up. He had tried and failed. But if he couldn't keep the family out of the water, at least he could stay out himself. They could all go in seven times seven if they wanted to—he wouldn't put his big toe in.

He didn't sleep well that night, his rest being interrupted by upsetting dreams. The dreams were inhabited by a strange being—the man he had seen surfing near the reef with the straw fedora on his head. In the dream, the man paddled to the shore with his tiny hands and it could be seen that he was smeared all over with an oily yellow liquid. There was no question what it was. Bill woke up sweating, then got up and stepped softly to the terrace, where he looked at the sea with loathing.

THE PREPARATIONS for the evening's celebration occupied most of the next day. There was the problem of wood for *las fogatas,* the smoke fires that would keep mosquitoes away. Rum, ice, glasses, towels, bathing suits, pots and pans, plus all the food, had to be packed. Huracán had to go down early to reserve the spot they always used—a spot, Bill saw with horror, very close to the drainpipe spouting sewage.

As darkness fell and they set out for the beach, joined now by relatives from Aibonito, Bill had the feeling that no one else understood the risks they were taking. At the same time, he wondered if he were exaggerating things. Doctors were prone to worry about illness, as Migdalia had pointed out this afternoon. They didn't have enough faith in the human body and in God.

The beach party got off to a fast start. Huracán had brought his bongos and they soon collected a crowd. The rum was passed freely. As usual, the Ramos fire was the biggest and the jolliest. Bill looked at Pipo, who had consented to sit in a beach chair this year in deference to his arthritis. His eyes were half shut and his face had a distant stubborn look. He reminded Bill of an aging sea-god.

Migdalia and Patricia had set up a pan for frying *bacalaítos*. The odor of the lard and the sound of the sizzling were wonderfully familiar to him. On how many occasions had he watched those little rounds of flour and codfish turn golden while the rum was passed around? On how many holidays had he heard the crisp sound of Puerto Rican Spanish? On how many San Juan Bautista eves had he lain on the warm sand while Huracán played the drums until it was time to put on their bathing suits and set forth on their seven journeys into the murmurous sea?

Perhaps he was drinking too much, but lying back under the stars that looked like holes punched in the sky, it seemed foolish not to drink, not to enjoy himself, not to revel in this fellowship. Someone started to sing a song that was his favorite, the *lamento borincano*. Its bittersweet words twined around him. In the distance he could hear Patricia warning his godson not to get too near the fire.

He must have dozed off, because he was suddenly aware of hands shaking him and grinning, of drunken faces peering down at him. He sat up, his head buzzing, and looked around. He could see dark shapes going past, heading for the water.

"*Vente.*" It was Pipo's voice. He was on his feet, wearing only a bathing suit. It was not a request, it was a command.

Bill shook his head. He would not go.

"*Vente!*" Pipo's voice was stronger now. Bill shook his head again.

He saw Migdalia get up and walk toward him. She seemed to have grown in stature—perhaps it was a trick of the firelight. She stood over him. "*Vente,*" she murmured, then more softly, "*mi hijo.*"

It was harder this time. She had called him her son. But he shook his head for a third time.

A voice he recognized as Huracán's cut in. "Let him alone, he doesn't wanna go in." He could see Huracán dancing away from the others, heading for the water. The rest were beginning to turn and follow him. A thin drumbeat of anxiety started in his chest.

"Si no vienes con nosotros," it was Migdalia again, *"no puedo echarte la bendición."*

The words opened in him like a wound. If he did not go with them, she would withhold her blessing. His heartbeat speeded up, but he still refused to answer.

And then he felt himself scooped up from behind by strong arms. It was Huracán and his friends. They had tricked him. He was being grabbed from all sides now, by six, eight of them, and carried toward the water. They were shouting and laughing as they raced over the sand, avoiding the obstacles, while the onlookers cheered. As he felt himself borne along he knew that he still might escape. If he kicked, thrashed, grew truly angry, they would let him go.

But he did not.

Water was splashing on him now, foaming all around.

"Okay!" cried Huracán, "now!" In a roar of voices he was dipped in water. The black liquid filled his mouth.

"Out!" commanded Huracán. They raced him back to the beach.

They turned and invaded the water and he was dipped again. Again... and again... the little squad carrying out Huracán's frenzied commands as if they were soldiers.

As he was passed back and forth from shore to sea, Bill gave in to a limpness that seemed to have taken complete possession of him. He no longer even wanted to resist.

At the seventh immersion, they dropped him in the water and swam off. Bill let himself float to the surface, then twisted over on his back and regarded the stars, which were weak and blurry due to the water in his eyes.

He swam slowly to shore and walked up to the fire. The

others looked at him sheepishly. Even Pipo seemed embarrassed. Patricia offered him a codfish cake, crisp and warm from the pan, but he shook his head and walked to the edge of the firelight, where he lay down in his wet clothes. Lightly he ran his tongue over his lips. He could taste salt. Whether it was the salt of the sea or of his vexatious tears, he wasn't sure. He only knew that under it was something oily and yellowish and foul...

THE FEVER CAME ON the day he expected it would. He had debated several times whether or not to go to the Outpatient Clinic of the Health Service for preventive shots. But each time he had rejected the notion. It seemed that the decision about illness, like the decision about going in the water, had been taken out of his hands.

The first day's discomfort was not great, and Migdalia pronounced it an attack of *la monga,* the tropical flu of the island. He took her advice, drank lots of liquid, and stayed in bed.

But by the second night his fever was too high for *la monga* and his joints felt as if they were being broken by sledge hammers. A doctor was called, a Cuban, who gave him penicillin. Bill wanted to reveal the true nature of his illness, but he thought the Cuban would not understand. Also, he sensed that it would be better to let his fate be decided by others. By doing so, he would learn something important about himself.

The crisis came that same night. Towards midnight the thrashing and sweating ceased and the room was filled with a blue light while his fingers became long and waxy, like candles. Everything appeared both near and blurred, as if seen through clear gelatin, and the middle-aged man with the fedora who had been surfing near the reef stepped through the wall of the bedroom. He approached Bill's bed by dancing a limber cha-cha, tucking his feet in and out as if he were on wheels. But as he came near, Bill saw that his eyes were not merry and festive but agate-hard and the cha-cha was not a dance of joy but a gesture of the most obscene triumph.

"*Mi casa es su casa,*" the little man said, twirling his body around.

Bill opened his eyes as wide as he could, although he was not surprised. He had always known that the angel of death would speak Spanish.

The man peered down at him. "*Mi casa es su casa,*" he repeated more fiercely.

The blue light grew stronger and gave off a crackling sound. Bill understood that he would have to speak up or lose his chance for good.

"No," he managed to say at last, struggling to a sitting position. "No!" he repeated, and then in English, loudly, "I was mistaken! Your house is not my house! It never was!"

The man glared at him angrily, then snapped his fingers. Quickly he turned and did his rubbery cha-cha toward the wall. Just before disappearing he looked around and hissed an obscenity in Spanish. Then he pinched his cheek in contempt and vanished. After that, only the trade wind could be heard, snuffling through the shutters.

After Bill's convalescence, and without telling anyone, he put the beach apartment on the market. He sold it a month later. He advised the new owner to have the locks changed.

In the North, that fall and winter, he saw the Ramos family only once, on Guillermo's birthday. When they asked why he didn't visit more often, he replied only that he had been busy. It was true. He had met a young man at a medical conference. The young man was named Victor Conroy and he was from Minneapolis. He worked as a lab technician and was exactly eight years younger than Bill. When Bill was not working, he was with Victor. They had begun to talk about sharing a flat.

It was clear from the beginning that Victor did not have the furious gift for life that the Puerto Ricans did—after all, he came from a caste-ridden, puritanical and anglified society. But Bill consoled himself by noting that in a certain light his lover's skin glowed with the warmth of a beach-fire on San

Juan Bautista eve, and his eyes shone with the silvery phosphorescence of waves as they broke over limestone reefs in tropic seas. At such times, with a sigh, Bill would reach out and clasp him fiercely, then insist on making love with a passion that Victor found alarming, since he could never quite understand the secret source of so much turbulence.

The Servant Problem

MEADE GAZED DOWN at the floor with distaste. Alan, his therapist, was already there, sitting cross-legged, holding up the goddam pillow. Meade knew that pillow. It was brown corduroy, with a zipper along one edge. Meade had punched it, caressed it, consoled it and once, in a fit of childish fury, bitten it. Alan had been especially pleased with the biting episode. He had nodded afterward, his handsome face creased with approval, and remarked, "Well, *that* got the anger out."

What Alan didn't know, and what Meade hadn't gotten up the nerve to tell him, was that the anger always built up again the next day. Just as bad as before. Worse. However, he didn't want Alan to think the therapy wasn't working. So at each session, when Alan murmured, "All right, let's work on the floor," Meade had slid unhappily downward, concealing his distaste, repressing his doubts about the whole procedure, and mangled the pillow according to instructions.

But today, his distaste was greater than ever. He had had a particularly bad time at the office, though that was nothing new. He had also had an unsatisfactory session with the trick sent over by his call-service last night. And to top it off, he had just quarreled with two of his best friends. Not a quarrel, really. They had simply begun to criticize him at dinner— maliciously, unfairly. He had listened to their slanders, his heart thumping and his forehead sweating, and found he was unable to defend himself. It was too shocking. A true betrayal, like Caesar with Brutus. At last, choking down his rage, he had flung down his napkin and walked out of Sonny's apartment. He had even walked all the way home—forty blocks from the upper East Side to lower Fifth Avenue, aware that his angina might flare up at any moment, to say nothing of the risk of muggers.

Alan was squatting on the floor, holding up the pillow. Waiting. Meade had the sudden impression that Alan was a trainer and he himself a broken-down fighter, doomed to punch the brown bag in a hopeless match forever.

He slid slowly down to the floor.

"Now," Alan half-closed his eyes, glimmering at him (a trick Meade found especially irritating). "Let's try to work on some of our anger again." Alan wiggled the pillow. "This is someone you hate."

"My assistant. That sneak."

"What's her name?"

"Sandra. She's trying to get my job. I think she's giving Morty blow jobs on the side."

Alan nodded. He had heard the passion and was pleased. "Go on, I want to hear you get angry."

Meade fished around in his insides, looking for some anger. Although he had been furious with Sandra today, he couldn't quite find it now. The anger seemed to have evaporated coming downtown on the subway.

"Goddamn you," he said. He glared at the pillow. It was quite frayed.

"I can't hear you."

"Trying to go over my head! Comptroller... don't make me laugh, you can hardly add two and two!"

"I still can't hear you."

Of course, words weren't enough. Alan expected him to *do* something. That was the point of gestalt therapy. You didn't lie around moaning and groaning about mommy and daddy. You had to act things out in the now.

Meade drove his fist into the pillow. It was foam rubber and sprang right back. "I'll kill you!"

"Listen to yourself. You're still calm. Your voice is absolutely even."

Oh God, he'd forgotten to raise his voice this time. He was so busy thinking about punching the pillow he had neglected his voice levels.

He raised his arm, ready to repeat the action, when suddenly the pillow, without his willing it, changed into the face of Sonny DeSaix and he was at the dinner party where they had attacked him so unfairly.

"You lousy rotten sonuvabitch!" he roared at Sonny, smashing him in the middle of his Roman-senator nose. "Go fuck yourself!" His surroundings faded as a storm of anger invaded him. At the same time his skin prickled and he knew his face was purpling up, the pits and scars deepening into bloody crescents. That meant his blood pressure was rising, a bad sign, but he couldn't help it. He had to lash back. "That's the last time you'll see me at your house!"

He grabbed the pillow and proceeded to strangle it. It felt amazingly good. Then he lifted it and banged it against the floor. That was what Sonny deserved. Sonny and Bart both. Who the fuck did they think they were?

"You are the most selfish person I've ever met," Sonny had said to him with the cold venom of an adder. *Selfish!* When it was he, Meade, who kept the crowd together! Gave the parties, bought the tickets, arranged the bridge games. Cooked the big meals at Christmas and Thanksgiving. And they called him selfish!

Suddenly he heard Bart chiming in, his voice high and whiny. "I can't stand your gossiping. You are so destructive. Everybody's afraid to tell you a thing. You know what we call you? *Central!*"

His blood ran cold at the nickname, even now. If he passed on information, it was never with malice. People wanted to hear news about other people. They confided in him because they expected him to pass it on. *Central!*

Suddenly the vision faded and he was aware of a knifelike

pain at the back of his head. "I have a headache," he announced.

However, Alan seemed to approve of headaches. "Do you want me to give you a massage?' he asked.

Meade looked at Alan warily. He didn't really know. He was exhausted. Suddenly he wished that he were talking to Elvira instead of to Alan. Elvira was his maid, a young woman with a cinnamon skin and a cool, unfathomable manner. She had been born in Trinidad. She came on Saturdays. He hadn't really begun to recover from the awful dinner party until he had spent the morning with Elvira. He couldn't discuss Sonny and Burt in detail with her, of course, but that wasn't necessary. Elvira cured simply by being in his apartment. Dusting. Cleaning. Ironing. Singing as she worked. After three hours with Elvira he was calm again. How strange it was. He had sometimes thought that Elvira, who barely knew how to read and write, had done more for him than all his therapists combined.

He refocused on Alan, who seemed to be moving toward him. He let Alan gentle him backwards until he lay full-length on his stomach. It was not really a comfortable position but he tried to make the best of it. Massage seemed to be an important part of gestalt too.

Alan was almost lying on top of him. Meade wished he wouldn't do that. He could hardly get his breath. Still, it felt good in a way. He could feel Alan's hard chest pressing against his kidneys. Then he sensed the outline of Alan's genitals against the back of his thigh. Alan was really quite attractive. He occasionally worked as a surrogate at one of the sex-therapy clinics. Suddenly Meade imagined that they were doing this in the nude. He wouldn't like Alan on top of his backside, of course. He would much prefer to have Alan under him. Or, even better, on his knees in front of him.

Alan's fingers dug into the hard, resistant patches of his neck and shoulders. His breath was loud and intimate in Meade's ears. At last, Meade went limp. He was really drained. At the same time, the screen of his mind went blank.

"Why don't we talk?" Alan's voice came from some distance away. Meade looked up groggily. Alan had moved to his easy chair. The massage was over.

It took him a while to pull himself off the floor, almost as if he had been pasted to it like a decal. His flesh felt leaden, paralyzed by gravity. But he was less tired now, amazingly, and his headache was gone. Alan was smiling broadly. "That wasn't all about Sandra," he said.

Meade nodded. "No, it was somebody else." He explained about the trouble with Sonny and Bart, noting for the hundredth time the inadequacy of explanations. However, he couldn't bring himself to tell Alan about Central. The pain was still too great.

"Do you think their criticisms were fair?"

Meade shook his head. "No." He explained about his cooking, his hospitality. Alan glimmered at him and Meade could tell he was skeptical. He had a sudden image of Alan, Sonny and Bart, all lined up against him and the heat began to mount to his cheeks again. Then he recalled Dexter Troop, his previous therapist. Dexter had never been skeptical. He had gone to Dexter because of an ad in the *Village Voice*. Dexter offered to rearrange energy patterns and unblock chakras. This, Meade discovered, involved mostly hot towels. "Just a moment," Dexter would say at moments of stress, "let's get a hot towel on that." Meade had finally stopped seeing Dexter because he realized the man had nothing to offer except some techniques picked up in the violent ward at Islip. Still, Dexter had never been skeptical.

"Could it be that you're introjecting again?"

That was one of Alan's favorite words. He thought everybody introjected a lot. "I don't think so. They were really very nasty. I didn't imagine it."

He tried to keep the sulk out of his voice with only partial success. Why didn't Alan support him, instead of criticizing him? Looking at Alan now, so trim and smug in his armchair, it occurred to Meade that Alan probably didn't require much comfort himself. The hard life for Alan. Alan had been recommended to him by a writer friend noted for an almost unearthly self-discipline. The writer could turn out a novel in six weeks and a short story in six hours. After a few months with Alan, the writer was down to four weeks for a novel and an hour for a short story.

"Nobody likes me," said Meade.

Alan looked at him balefully. "That's pure shit and you know it."

Meade glared back. What did Alan know about the need for comfort? For love? What did Alan know about something as simple as eating, for example?

Last year Meade had gone to a food therapist. This man, who had a fancy office on Park Avenue, used suggestion and hypnosis to get his patients to stop overeating. This had helped Meade, but the fee was $60 an hour and he couldn't really afford it. His weight had soared as soon as he stopped going.

"I want you to say that again and really hear what you're saying. 'Nobody likes me.' "

Alan was infuriating. They were all infuriating, really. All except Elvira. At the thought of Elvira, his anger receded slightly. If only she were coming tomorrow instead of next Saturday! If only he could afford to have her around three days a week instead of one! He had told Alan about Elvira, but he hadn't understood. Of course not. Such relationships were entirely outside the range of Alan's experience.

Alan was eyeing the floor and Meade jerked his head back. He knew what Alan was thinking. More bullshit with the pillow. The silence alarmed him. Meade took a deep breath.

"You're right. It isn't true that nobody likes me. There is somebody." Alan, he noted, looked interested. "His name is Peter. Peter Pride." He paused, then added, "I don't think that's his real name. He uses it . . . um, professionally."

Alan, of course, didn't approve of hustlers. Alan had a lover named Vinny—they had been together for nine years. Although they were no longer monogamous, Alan had informed him that each was the other's "primary person." This was said during their first interview, before treatment began. In gestalt therapy you got to know something about your counselor's private life. Meade liked this openness, but at the same time had gotten the impression that Alan was bragging. Nine years with the same lover. It all reminded him of the Freudian analyst he had gone to fifteen years earlier, when he was still in his twenties. The Freudian kept a color photo of his wife and children on his desk. The gender was different nowadays, but the idea seemed to be the same.

"Yes, Peter Pride. I met him ... well ... the usual way. But he isn't like the other boys. He wants to be an actor. I'm going to help him. I've got contacts."

Alan was beginning to look disapproving. Meade hurried on.

"He's been over three ... four ... times. Spent the night. I didn't sleep at all, just hugged him all night long."

His frame heaved at the memory. It was true. Each time, Peter had arrived about eleven o'clock. They had stripped quickly and begun to make feverish love. Peter was 24, a native of West Germany. He had none of the American hang-ups about status and sex. He would do anything. Afterwards he slung his long-limbed body, the color of clover honey, onto the bed and, when Meade got out of the shower, entwined his legs around Meade's like a boa. After that, Peter would drop off to sleep while Meade stayed awake, secretly running his fingers up and down Peter's flawless skin. It was a sensation he could never get enough of. He would lie in the dark, steeping himself in the splendor of that silky integument, refining the world down to one absorbing sensation in his fingers as the hours ticked by and he fought off sleep. Each morning, after a night with Peter, he had felt marvelously refreshed, as if he had spent the hours under a waterfall of milk. His own body seemed remade, his damaged skin made whole, by the perfection of Peter.

He always gave Peter a little extra something in the morning, over and above the regular fee.

"What would happen if you met someone and didn't pay him?"

He'd been steeling himself for this question. "I'd be delighted. I just can't get the people I like without paying."

"Have you tried?"

He thought about his trips to the bars, the baths, the waterfront. Oh, there had been offers. He wasn't all that unattractive, in spite of his extra weight and gray hair. But there hadn't been anyone like Peter. "Sure I've tried," he replied.

"Are you sure it's Peter's looks that appeal to you? Maybe you like to pay."

He'd heard that one before too. He didn't even bother to answer. It was ridiculous.

"I'm having a fantasy I'd like to share with you," Alan said.

Meade settled back, casting a sidelong glance at the clock. Just another ten minutes, thank God.

"My fantasy involves you and someone your own age who doesn't look like a movie star..."

As Alan unreeled his images, Meade turned his mind aside. Absurd to think he could get interested in someone his own age. Besides, other men in their forties were mostly after youngsters. As Alan droned on, his eyes glimmering, Meade embarked on a fantasy of his own. It involved both Peter Pride and Elvira. He had summoned up a charming ménage for the three of them. Something bucolic—the Berkshires, perhaps—but with all the latest conveniences, including a Cuisinart. Elvira would work all day at housekeeping chores while he and Peter skinny-dipped in a clear mountain stream. After that he would ask Peter to suck him off while Elvira stood around offering rum-and-lime concoctions from her native island.

"What do you think of that?"

He blinked rapidly. He hadn't heard a word Alan had said. "I think it's... unrealistic," he said thoughtfully. "Totally unrealistic."

Alan looked miffed and the image of Elvira, Peter and himself slipped back into Meade's mind. He had left out the best part. At the end of each day, they would have a treasure hunt. He would hide jeweled Easter eggs under shrubs and rocks so that they would have the pleasure of discovering them. After each trove was found, they would run to him to express their gratitude. He would pretend it was nothing, even though the eggs had cost him a thousand dollars each.

"I'm afraid you're the unrealistic one, Meade. That's why you get so little satisfaction out of life." Alan searched his face. "What are you thinking about now?" he demanded.

Overcoming his reluctance, Meade told him about the cottage in the Berkshires. He went from that to the Easter egg hunt, becoming more excited as he went along. He could feel Alan's eyes boring into him, but he refused to be intimidated. Alan's spartan life didn't qualify him to judge needs like his own. Alan had no true understanding of people who required extra love and support. A dull anger boomed in his chest, quite different from the violence he had felt toward Sonny and Bart a while ago. This anger seemed directed not only at Alan but at someone larger and less well-defined—perhaps at his grandmother, who had stroked his cheek when he was adolescent, predicting that his acne would disappear and that he would grow up to be a handsome man; perhaps at his father, who had given him mountains of toys after a big win at gambling, but had been morose and withdrawn the rest of the time; perhaps at his boy-cousins, lumpy with muscles, who had run in and out of his childhood scoring touchdowns and home runs without half trying. Could therapy undo memories like these? Did he even want it to?

"Is it possible that all the people in this cottage that you fantasize are really your servants? That you can only trust people who are totally dependent on you?"

What did that mean exactly? Did it have any meaning at all? Oh yes, rolled up somewhere in those words, a red dot at the center like a pimento in an olive, was a meaning of some sort. But it had nothing to do with him, with Meade

Carandelle, who had spent more than four decades looking for enough truth to get him through each day.

"We have to work on this some more. Your servant problem."

"My servant problem!" The words burst out of him with surprising force. "It isn't my problem at all . . . it's more like yours!"

Alan smiled in a superior way and Meade knew he hadn't explained, hadn't done justice to the richness of his thought. And then a bright space opened directly in front of him and in it he discerned therapists as far ahead as he could see, an avenue of bearded sphinxes past which he would be carried like a mummy to his tomb, unless he could understand deeply and truly the nature of his attachments. And he saw that in a sense Alan was right—the servant problem *was* his problem, but not in the way that Alan thought.

"I do not believe," he paused, shuddering at the energy that flew along his tongue, "that love is all give and take. One way is enough." He paused and a brief tremor shook him again. *"Either* way is enough."

Was that what he wanted to say? Was that it exactly? He thought about Elvira and Peter, seeing them exactly as they were—self-centered, greedy, manipulative. But he had always known that about them, known it to the deepest level of his self.

Alan was glimmering at him again. "It's important not to rationalize the inability to have meaningful . . ." Meade didn't hear the rest of the sentence. It didn't matter—he'd been hearing that sentence in various forms for most of his life.

Yes, they were self-centered. Takers. Users. But did it matter? Really?

"Love is not a two-way street." The words seemed to push out of his mouth with a life of their own. "You don't have to reciprocate. I mean," he corrected himself, *"they* don't have to."

Alan was off and running now with a description of his nine years with Vinny. They had shared many things, but the most beautiful thing they had shared was sharing itself. Meade had the sudden image of their life together as an apple pie which had been cut exactly in half.

"But that's not what I want."

Alan stopped his recital and tilted his head, looking at him as a bird might look at a worm. "Of course you do. You just can't let yourself believe in it."

"As far as I'm concerned, one night with Peter is worth nine years with Vinny!"

"Will you feel that way next week? When Peter's gone and you're all by yourself? You're always complaining about being lonely."

It was true. Some nights the loneliness in his bedroom enveloped him like a shroud. He could hardly breathe. He struggled against the memory, trying to regain the sense of new vistas, new hope, he had had just a few minutes ago. But it was hard. Alan's studio, the shag rug, the hateful brown pillow, all seemed to close down on him. He could see nothing ahead but more sessions like this one.

And then, suddenly, he heard a voice. It was soft and lilting, with an accent he recognized as West Indian. "Run for de doctor," it crooned, "tell him to come as quick as he can." He turned sharply, holding his breath. Was it coming from the next apartment?

Alan stood up. "I'm afraid our time is up."

Meade remained seated as Alan shifted impatiently. "It was a good session, Meade, we'll have to work on this some more."

At last Meade hoisted himself up, trying not to wobble. Would the voice sound again? Would there be further communication? "Yeah," he mumbled, "it was a good session."

At the door he half-turned. The room was quiet. Alan's hand was on the lock. And then, ever so faintly, he heard the voice again: "Mama don't want no peas and rice and coconut oil." He winced at the sudden pain in his chest. The voice belonged to Elvira.

"Are you okay? You want to sit down for a minute?"

Alan's hand was on his arm, but he shook his head and brushed it away. If he was going to have an angina attack he would rather have it outside.

"I'm okay." With a last nod, he shuffled into the hall, holding the wall for support. He knew Alan was watching but he didn't look back.

He walked slowly down Fifth Avenue, taking long rest stops. The pain in his chest had subsided to a dull ache. He kept his hand pressed there while he thought about the voice. Had he been hallucinating? Had Elvira been singing calypso songs in his head? It was bizarre—just the sort of thing he hated. On the other hand, the walls in that building were paper thin. Perhaps a phonograph had been playing in the next apartment and the voice had reminded him of Elvira's.

But even as he explained away the sound, he felt disappointed. If it hadn't been Elvira, then there had been nothing special about the session with Alan. It had been a failure, like all the others. He suddenly felt bleak. Nothing in his life had changed. Nothing would ever change. Looking around the streets now, at the New Yorkers with their sour faces and gray skins, he saw that tomorrow would bring all the usual troubles. It would be another rotten day. His heart gave another painful tug but this time he didn't stop to rest. That wouldn't help either. And it didn't matter. There was nothing ahead but endless sessions with Alan or with someone else just like him.

A stranger in a leather jacket was sitting on the front stoop of his house. He was tall and well made, with a broad smiling face under tawny hair. It was Peter Pride. Peter was waiting for him!

"Hello, Meade," Peter said cheerily. He pronounced it *Meet*. "I came to see how you are." Peter laughed at that, a dumb happy laugh, and Meade knew that Peter probably had no place else to spend the night. Still, that didn't keep his pulse from jumping nor a mindless joy from racing through him.

"Well come in," he said.

Peter towered over him as he unlocked the downstairs door, then the apartment door. As he fiddled with the key, Meade was deliciously aware of Peter's presence, of the smell of leather and Aramis, of the promise of adventure to come. Inside, before turning on the light, he grabbed Peter and hugged him tightly. The young man's body seemed a splendid thing, a feast of the flesh from which he had been absent too long. He registered the depth of Peter's chest, the slimness of his waist, the weight of his thighs, as his own face flushed and his blood pressure mounted another notch. But he didn't worry about that. He was free of care, free of the past, at least for now.

He propelled Peter into the bedroom and they began to undress. As Peter took off his shirt, Meade had the impression that nothing was real or true outside this room, outside the drama of their disrobing. And then, as Peter stepped from his briefs, his body blazing like a sun, something unclenched in Meade's chest and he saw quite clearly that only silly people could fail to understand that a loving servant was worth his weight in gold. That, in fact, love was not something you had to earn through good behavior or self-denial, rather like a parole from jail, but something you needed only the courage to ask for, from anyone nearby. And that it was not love that had failed him in the past, but merely the courage to ask for it. Love was simply another gift you gave yourself.

They lay down on the bed and he spent a long time running his fingers across Peter's chest, which was a smooth coverlet of shining moiré silk. Peter kept his eyes closed while this was going on, his lips tilted in a blissful smile. Peter loved the attention, Meade knew, loved being worshiped. And Meade saw Peter's happiness as his own, Peter's participation as unlimited, despite the fact that Peter did nothing but lie very still, smiling.

And then, echoing very faintly in the bedroom, he heard a familiar voice. It was smooth and silky, rather like Peter's skin, and it lapped around him gently. "When my money run out I'd have no regret," it crooned, "I'll buy some of everything that money can get."

"Right on, Elvira," Meade giggled to himself. Then he began to lick Peter all over, rather like an ice-cream cone, deliciously oblivious to what his therapist—or any therapist—would care to say about the nature of his need.

The Household God

Albert always picked up the mail himself, or he would not have taken a chance on answering the ad. He arrived home from school at four, a good two hours ahead of Scott, who kept office hours for patients from four to six. Even so, as the time for a reply drew near, Albert found himself getting nervous. The thought that Scott might arrive first and find the letter gave him a jolt of panic. The whole thing was a breach of faith—faith in Scott, in their life together. By mailing the application to New Friends, Inc., by putting his desire down in black and white, he had released something new in life. He didn't really like new things. At forty-six he understood the value of routine.

Several times, as he and Scott were eating dinner at the big oak table (too big for two people, really), he had been swept by the desire to confess. It would have been so easy. Scott would have nodded his craggy head with the jutting chin, and his mocha eyes would have darkened as he touched his mustache. How well he knew that quick nod, the look that said, you can't surprise *me*, Albie. There was no secret they couldn't share. Sharing put everything in its proper place, like an item on the whatnot shelf in the parlor.

Yes, he could have told Scott everything. What hadn't they talked about! Their infidelities, for instance—in twelve years they had both succumbed to temptation at regular intervals. Still, their bond remained strong, unbroken. It couldn't be broken simply because it could always be brought up for inspection—its sturdiness tested, its frayed edges mended through the healing power of honest talk.

But now, for the first time, he didn't want to share the secret. In fact—the thought struck him as he watched Scott ladle peanut soup from the Spode tureen they had bought in St. Thomas last year—talking it over would have ruined it. They would have found a place for it where it didn't belong— in their restored Victorian house on Pacific Heights, among the candelabra with the crystal pendants, the prints from *Godey's Lady's Book* and the side-chairs upholstered in red velvet. As he pulled the tureen toward him, the traitorous thought struck him that it was to escape from these beloved things that he had written to New Friends, Inc. in the first place.

The reply arrived the following Wednesday. Driving home from school—he taught social studies at a high school down on the peninsula—he had gotten caught in a massive traffic jam and been delayed. It was almost six when he opened the front door and saw the envelope lying on the floor. His stomach tensed convulsively. Ten minutes later and Scott would have been the one to pick it up.

He took the letter into the library at the back of the house, a room with tall bookcases overlooking the garden, where he did his reading and schoolwork. It was an orderly place, full of precious things. As usual, his glance went first to the small model of Zeus Thunderer on the desk. The old god seemed stern and powerful this evening, the empty eye-sockets full of menace in the fading light. He had bought that reproduction in Athens last summer, after seeing the original in the Archaeological Museum. Now, glancing at the muscular figure with the sightless eyes and poised thunderbolt, he repressed a tremor. There seemed to be an unpleasant connection between that statue and the envelope in his hand.

As he slit the envelope open, he heard the distant creak of the garage doors. Scott was putting his Mercedes away. He just had time to scan the letter. The typing was neat and professional.

"We have run a computer match with our subscriber list and we are happy to inform you that we have found an exciting New Friend for you—someone who meets your physical specifications and shares your special tastes. His name is Jim."

The front door slammed. He called out a hello. Scott's reply was mild and tired.

"Clipped to this letter is the insignia which will identify you. Please wear it in your lapel at your first meeting, which will be on Saturday at 5 P.M. at the Tiger on Folsom Street. Jim will wear the same insignia."

He just had time to glance at the red metal disk and to note the two joined hands before Scott's heavy footsteps reached the door of the library. He folded the letter and slid it quickly into a Greek lexicon on the lower shelf.

"Hi." Scott's kiss was perfunctory.

"How are you this evening?"

Scott shook his head. "Whole goddam city has the flu." He looked around the room without interest. "Any mail?"

Albert shook his head. "No, nothing." He pushed his glasses back nervously. The lie had taken him by surprise.

"What about eating out?"

"Suits me just fine. I was late getting home."

After Scott had changed, they went to a vegetarian place on Polk Street. They both ordered tabbouleh and a spinach quiche. As he watched Scott eat—he was wearing a Guatemalan poncho with an intricate design—it occurred to him that Scott looked quite worn, older than forty-eight. The seams in his forehead were deep, the skin around his eyes folded in layers. Of course, Scott had been working too hard lately—at the hospital before eight in the morning, on a mayor's committee for VD control, a volunteer at a clinic in the Mission District on weekends. All this was in addition to his private practice. But there was nothing he, Albert, could do. His warnings would be shrugged off. Scott seemed to need the heavy routine, as if it were a disguise of some sort. And it had been getting worse in the past half year—thicker and more impenetrable.

Again he thought about telling Scott of his contact with New Friends, Inc. It struck him that it wouldn't be too hard to put the responsibility onto Scott. They hadn't had much fun together recently—in bed or out of it. Scott's fatigue had curled around their life like the fog that oozed under the Golden Gate Bridge each afternoon. But again he let the opportunity pass.

After dinner they took a walk up Polk Street. Neither spoke much. It seemed quite uninteresting to Albert. The few attractive people they passed gave them only brief glances. It was clear how they looked—a middle-aged married couple. When they reached home, Scott flipped on the TV and sank into the gentleman's chair. As the screen lit, he lowered his eyelids. Albert could see he was getting ready for a nap. Not so long ago, he wouldn't have minded. Now he did.

Stifling his annoyance, he went back to the library. A pile of *New Yorker*s had accumulated. Perhaps he would make a dent in them. He began flipping through the glossy pages without reading, aware of the comfort that the ads transmitted. How well he knew this beautiful world! How soothing was the sight of all this well-ordered luxury!

But even as the magazine smoothed away his irritation, he was aware of another impulse. The promise of these pages was a fraud—it could provide no real satisfaction. He had a sudden image of *The New Yorker* as a map to a territory that didn't really exist—a place as ideal as Montsalvat, as elusive as Shangri-La. Allowing it to influence him all these years, years of buying furniture and clothes and books, had made his life as slick as the pages themselves. As slick and orderly and boring.

He threw the issue angrily aside and glanced at the Zeus. The thunderbolt had caught a gleam of light from the lamp. The metal point seemed tipped with fire. For one mad instant the whole construction came alive and it seemed as if the old god might hurl the metal shaft. Almost on cue, the hotel room on Miltiadou Street came back to him. He saw again the high ceiling and sepia walls and heavy furniture. He and

Scott had arrived in Athens at night, exhausted from the long plane trip. But when they reached their room, they had found a sight waiting for them that had refreshed them instantly. It was the Acropolis, floodlit for summer, framed in the window of their room. Albert's breath came short now, remembering. They hadn't bothered to unpack—just sat at the window, staring at the white marble columns, the bleached bones of Greece on their ancient catafalque. Then, without speaking, they had moved to the bed, undressing as they went. The time had come to celebrate something they could not name.

Scott's body seemed harder and firmer that night, in spite of the extra weight around his middle. Perhaps it was a trick of the reflected light, but when Albert skimmed his fingers over the skin, he felt he was touching a statue sculpted by a master. As they lay down and he took Scott in his arms, the bones seemed longer, the chest deeper, the arms and legs more massive. Albert had the feeling he was holding a stranger—someone whose contours were unfamiliar and full of unexplored mystery.

They had lain quietly for a time, soaking up the presences in the room, and then it had started. Slowly at first, then building gradually until they had both given way to it—the same deep urge in each man to impose his will on the other. Over and around they went, twisting and grunting as they scrabbled for a hold, struggled to gain mastery, while their breath came hoarse and their faces turned red. Perhaps it was the fatigue of the plane trip, or the time change, or the sight of the Parthenon, but Albert had never felt like this, had never seen Scott so possessed, had never dueled with him on this kind of battlefield. It seemed, as they rolled over and over, that they were fighting to find something they had always missed, some final truth that only the aching flesh could reveal. Finally, Scott straddled him and stared at him from a face that was dark and unreadable. Then Scott reared back and, as Albert struggled to a half-sitting position, gave him a powerful blow on the cheek with his open hand. Albert had gone limp at that—limp with pain and shock—and then he had thrown himself at Scott, knocking him backward and shouting curses as he forced him down, down, under his chest, under his belly, his groin... Then suddenly, at the same instant, the anger left them. "My God, Albie," Scott struggled to a sitting position, "what happened?" His eyes were full of grief. He himself had been too shaken to answer, just moved aside while a shudder of remorse went through his body. They had gotten up without speaking again and gone to sleep without reaching orgasm.

The sound of the television intruded into his thoughts. He could imagine Scott slumped in the chair, deaf to the commercial. How long ago that night in Athens seemed! Did he really imagine that Scott was full of unexplored mystery? That they might pummel their way through the doors of the flesh to some new revelation—at their age?

He shook his head, then glanced toward the statue. Suddenly it struck him that the Zeus was really like the ads in *The New Yorker*—fakey and slick. A slight depression seized him. He had brought home not a household god but another piece of furniture. Their trip to Greece had actually been a failure. They had spent the ten days doing all the right things, but nothing had caught fire. It had been a disappointment. They had missed, right from the beginning.

He went to bed that evening with the depression still on him. His tongue tasted like a bathing slipper. He slept poorly, dreaming that he was in a foreign country and had lost his way.

On Saturday morning, he mentioned casually that he had been invited to another teacher's home for drinks that afternoon. He knew that Scott, though invited, wouldn't come. He hated shoptalk about education. But he needn't have lied. Scott's schedule at the Saturday clinic had been changed. He had to be there all afternoon.

Albert chose his clothing for the afternoon date at the Tiger with great care. He didn't want to be typecast. After much thought, he put on a pair of worn jeans, a stud belt and a white Saint-Laurent shirt with a star pattern. He checked his appearance in the *armoire à glace* he had bought at the Spreckels auction. Not bad—not bad at all. His face was firm, his chin line strong, his blue eyes clear behind the contacts. Only the eyebrows, prematurely white, gave a clue to his age. He had often thought about dyeing them the same sandy color as his hair, but had never gotten around to it. He didn't put the insignia—the red button with the joined hands—into his lapel until he got in the car.

As he drove, he noticed that his hands were shaking, which surprised him. A few minutes later, he realized he was having trouble controlling the wheel. He slowed down, thinking this would help. Then, unaccountably, reflected in the windshield, he saw the first page of the application form from New Friends, Inc. He tried to look around it, but the page moved with his vision. It seemed to be accusing him.

What is your preferred sexual type? Please be specific about age, height, weight, complexion, body hair, etc.

He twisted his gaze away, but the page followed him again.

What parts of your body are most sensitive? Least sensitive? What parts of other bodies turn you on the most?

He jumped the light at Market and another driver cursed him, but he paid no attention.

What kind of action do you prefer? Genital? Anal? Oral? Other? If Other please describe.

As he looked for a parking spot on Folsom, his handwritten answers flashed into his mind. I prefer men of medium height, strongly built, with facial hair. Age is unimportant.

His answer to the second question had been brief. My whole body is sensitive, from head to toe.

But it was the third question that gave him the most trouble, as he knew it would. Before writing his answer, he had looked into the empty eyes of the Zeus for a long time. Then the words had slid off the tip of his pen as if they had been waiting there for ages. *I want a partner who will be my opponent. I want to struggle with him until we arrive someplace we've never been before. I think a certain kind of anger can turn you into a god.*

He had sealed the envelope quickly after that, and run out to the mailbox before he could change his mind.

Now, as he pushed open the door of the bar, his nervousness intensified, accompanied by a feeling of futility. How silly he had been! How childish! He was really too old for this kind of thing.

The interior was checkered with afternoon light. There were only a few patrons, squinting to look at him. His gaze went quickly to their lapels. No red buttons.

He went to the end of the bar and ordered a beer, chugging it at once. After the third swig he checked his watch. It was exactly five. He would give it five minutes and no more. Five minutes to prove he hadn't copped out, then...

The front door opened. A bearded man of middle height with a square head entered. He was in his early forties. He was wearing an Air Force jacket and levis. Albert heard a thin drumbeat start up in his chest. As soon as the man stepped out of the light he would be able to see his lapel.

"What are you doing here?" The voice came from another direction—behind him. He hadn't noticed anyone back there.

He turned quickly. The red button winked at him malevolently. He moved to cover his own lapel—too late.

"My God," the familiar craggy face stared at him. "It was you."

"You should have used your own name," he replied. Then he waited until he heard the sound of a thunderbolt being loosed in the deeps of his mind. After that he put down his beer with a trembling hand and said, "Let's go home. We've wasted too much time already."

The Judgment of Midas

FRANCIS BURNS had an early dinner alone. He moved around the little kitchen quickly and ate rapidly, almost angrily, barely tasting the food. After washing up, he went to the piano and began to pick out the Cavatina from *Faust*. It was an aria he didn't much like, but his fingers seemed to want to play it. Gradually, as the notes swelled, forming turrets and castles in E-flat, his pleasure and concentration grew, so that by the time he reached the second cadence he was humming along, his anger at the solitary meal and empty apartment quite forgotten. This Cavatina was the first piece he had played as an accompaniment for Charles, and performing it now he could almost feel Charles' heavy thigh pressing against his own on the piano bench. It was a foolish notion, since Charles had moved out a year ago, but still it gave him pleasure.

After finishing, he glanced at the clock. It took eighteen minutes to walk from his apartment to the opera house at Lincoln Center. He hated to arrive early. As a critic, he spent so much time in concert halls that to arrive early seemed unnecessary and unprofessional.

His hands splayed idly over the keys again, testing some chords until they sounded a familiar progression. A descending movement, A-flat, B, B-flat, resolving through the diminished to E. Wagner, of course. That downward slither, so oddly affecting even after thirty years of listening, belonged to Wotan and the fire music. Charles had never quite managed the *Abschied,* even after years of study, in spite of long hours working together right at this piano. For a moment, Francis imagined that he was correcting Charles' diction for the hundredth time: *Leb' wohl, du kühnes, herrliches, Kind!* German gave Charles a lot of trouble, and vice versa. When Francis found himself pronouncing the words carefully aloud, he took his hands from the keys and stood up.

He decided to wear his gray suit with a striped shirt and maroon tie tonight. He made it a point to dress carefully for the opera. He disapproved of people who wore casual clothes to the Metropolitan. Nowadays, the upper rings were filled with sloppy young people in denims—thrift-shop battalions who looked terribly out of place on those carpeted stairs and under the starburst chandeliers.

Charles had been the same way. When they had gone to an opening night a few years ago, Charles had wanted to wear his eternal bush jacket. Only after an unpleasant scene had Charles agreed to wear a jacket and tie. Charles had wandered through the lobbies at intermission, observing the gala crowd with a disapproving expression in his dark raccoon eyes. They were phonies, he informed Francis, to which Francis had replied that young people were too quick to judge. "Yeah?" Charles had replied, his dark eyes glittering, "you're here to judge, aren't you? And you even get paid for it."

The walk to Lincoln Center this evening was chilly, and Francis buttoned his coat against a cutting wind. It was not a pleasant part of town. The huge buildings at 66th Street seemed out of tune with their neighbors, which were seedy bars and decayed pharmacies. That was New York for you. One block glorious, the next tumbledown. He still found this rather exciting, however, although he had been here twenty years, almost half his life.

By the time Francis settled into his seat in the twelfth row, it was just after eight. To his surprise, the orchestra members had still not come in. Perhaps it had something to do with the special nature of the evening. It was not an opera performance but a gala benefit, featuring the two reigning prima donnas of the company. No doubt one of them was having an attack of temperament in her dressing room.

He opened the program. The orchestra would first play the prelude to *Meistersinger,* then Fiora Luigini would offer a solo, followed by Irena Vlamis. After that, another orchestral selection and more solos. The first half would end with the first-act duet from *Lakmé.*

Some oboists were filing in now, looking dyspeptic. Francis recalled the press release mailed to him at the newspaper. This was the first time the two divas were to blend their voices in public. A notable event, he thought, but hardly worth the hundred dollar top they were charging.

At last the crystal chandeliers started their dizzy ascent to the ceiling—the world's most expensive yo-yos—and the house lights dimmed. At the same moment it occurred to Francis that the evening's entertainment might be viewed as a song contest. That was a dangerous metaphor, of course, and might provoke invidious comparisons, but still it appealed to him. It was dramatic. It would make good reading. As the great C major chord of the *Meistersinger* prelude sounded (at last), Francis decided to use it as a lead for his review. He took out his little spiral notebook and began to write. The prelude tonight heralded a song contest not on the banks of the Pegnitz but along the Hudson. It was really a grander river by far.

When the prelude ended, the curtains opened to reveal a stage banked with flowers. There was a long pause, then Luigini swept in, looked dazed at the storm of applause. She was a big woman, without a waistline, whose body reminded Francis of a ship's funnel. She was wearing a gown of red velvet with long sleeves. Her best feature was her skin. It was rich and creamy, contrasting violently with her dark hair, now arranged in long, Medusa-like tresses. She squeezed her eyes at the crowd, then threw back her head and spread her legs slightly. The opening bars of the fourth-act air from *Trovatore* resounded.

She sang it well, but cautiously, Francis thought, taking

care with the phrases, floating the tones thoughtfully, not trying for a true pianissimo. Her diction was better than usual. After finishing, she swept girlishly off to warm applause, her ankles visible as she held up the skirt of her red gown, her head thrown back coquettishly.

Vlamis appeared almost at once, looking cool and secretive. This, Francis knew, was part of her dramatic technique—to seem aloof until the big moments, when she would go suddenly mad onstage, turning from chaste goddess to tigerish female. Tonight she moved smoothly to stage center, as if on wheels, and did not acknowledge the applause. Her eyes were flat and oval; Francis had seen the same eyes looking out of mosaics in the upper recesses of Hagia Sophia. She was dressed in a white sheath that accentuated her height and dark skin.

As she began the "Dove sono" he realized she was not in good voice. The tone was edgy and unfocused. Mozart's long legatos did not hold. He could see, from the play of her cheeks and jaw, from the tension in her shoulders, that she was trying to compensate, trying to bring her voice under control. To his surprise, he found himself secretly rooting for her. The da capo went better and the coda was quite passable.

The audience response was restrained, in spite of a few well-timed shouts from her claqueurs, the best in the business. But Francis felt strangely excited, as if he and Vlamis had overcome some obstacle together. He tried to dismiss this feeling—it was unprofessional—but still it lingered. He noticed that his palms were wet and his heart was pounding. Vlamis did not appear bothered by the cool reception. She inclined her head once, then wheeled off without looking back.

As the orchestra started up—it was the ballet music from *Faust,* which he detested—Francis found that he was still keyed up. Well, singing always did that to him. From the very beginning, when he was ten years old and his grandparents had brought the first Victor Red Seal records to his house. Lucrezia Bori and Giovanni Martinelli and Lily Pons and Beniamino Gigli—all those scratchy sounds played on the Magic Eye phonograph with its daring drop mechanism had altered his life forever. He had moved from the flat plains of Texas to a heaven guarded by the keepers of exotic keys like C-sharp and B minor. A music nut, right from the beginning. There was no help for it. His father would arrive home from the bank to find his son pale and nervous at the side of the greenly-glowing Magic Eye, barely able to greet him. His two years of bedwetting dated from the advent of the opera records.

And it was his passion for the human voice that had been the binding force in his relationship with Charles, whom he had met at the bar right in this house, during the second intermission of *Carmen*. Charles was a singer, and when Francis learned this—they were in bed together that same evening—it had seemed a vital, preordained connection with his deepest, truest self. A tiny pain lanced his side now and he knotted his hands as Gounod's cottony chords filled his ears. In the three years they had lived together he had let go completely. Unpeeled the outer skin that had protected him, for the first time in his life. Well, he would never do that again. Never let himself be seduced a second time into that pain and loss. Not for Charles, not for any singer.

The crowd's roar took him out of his reverie. The *Faust* excerpt had ended without his noticing and Luigini was back onstage. She had changed to a ball gown of blue silk, and seemed to have thickened even more in order to fill it up. She exuded, Francis thought, vast confidence and a kind of decayed voluptuousness. The shouting continued until she squeezed her eyes for quiet. As the orchestra started up—it was the big scene ending the first act of *Traviata*—she filled her mighty chest and spread her legs wide. The action seemed almost obscene, as if she were going to give birth in public, and Francis wondered for a moment if he should turn his head away. At the same time, he knew that she was going to sing magnificently.

And she did. She seemed to have turned back the pages of

the years so that her voice was bright with youth. He heard none of the vagaries of recent seasons—no scooping, no wobble, no uncertainty—just a purity of tone, a flawless glister through which the pitch shone true. When she started the cabaletta, he had the notion that her voice was a live thing, a creature existing inside her like an animal in the cave of the winds, and she had simply permitted it to come forth. It was all so natural. She took the closing runs sensuously, her eyes squeezed shut and her head tilted to one side, and found the high C easily. When she finished, she looked at the audience in lewd amazement, as if they had participated in an orgy together. At that moment, he thought, she was scarcely human.

He did not stir when the cheering started but sat very still, his hand cupped over his ear, as if he might preserve the rich sounds a moment longer. As if—the image came to him quite incongruously—he might press against the notes, might be warmed and comforted by them. At last, feeling unpleasantly drained, he joined in the applause.

There was a long wait before Irena Vlamis reappeared. Francis wondered if she had become upset by the sound of cheering. It was a thought that sent a pang through him. Again he found himself secretly rooting for her, and tried to dismiss the urge as unprofessional. But when she appeared at last, she seemed as before. Her obsidian eyes were flat and expressionless, her generous mouth carved in an arc of disdain. She stood very straight—she had not changed from her white sheath—until the house quieted down. Then she nodded and the "Casta diva" started.

Francis was disappointed to find that her vocal production was even poorer than before. The sound was shrill, the pitch uncertain. As the aria progressed, things grew worse. She went from sharp to flat. Her breath was not being parceled out correctly; the Bellini line was choppy and distorted. His disappointment changed to despair—she seemed to be doing nothing right. Then, as the music built to a series of high B's, her breath faltered and the last few notes came out cracked and harsh. Francis shrank from the sound. He had never heard Vlamis sing like that before.

And then her hands clenched, her shoulders stiffened and a fierce look came into her eyes. She was summoning her last reserves, he could see, and then, like a flame newly regulated, her voice steadied. He held his breath, aware of the pounding of his pulse. Perhaps... perhaps it would be all right. The second stanza began to unroll more fluidly, the voice under better control, the tones centered. When the high notes came around, she produced them well, without seeming effort, her arms sculpting the air gracefully. The audience did not interrupt with applause and she sailed into the cabaletta, gathering power as she went so that the scale came out crisply and beautifully. Just at the end, he put his opera glasses up. He could see that she was sweating heavily through her makeup but that her black eyes were dilated with joy. A feeling of enormous relief surged through him. She had managed after all.

The applause was thin and polite but Francis wasn't surprised. Audiences liked perfection. They didn't understand the expense of spirit needed to achieve it, nor the pain required to sustain it. But Vlamis, he was happy to see, didn't mind. She stood still, her hands at her sides, her head lowered humbly. Francis thought it was an attitude of utter triumph. Then, in a burst of elation, he realized that the soprano's performance was even greater for having almost missed. What was art, after all, but a victory over weakness and disorder? By rising above human infirmity, Vlamis had made it to the last full measure, to the end of the song. What could be finer or more beautiful than that? Suddenly Francis began to clap loudly. The people nearby glanced at him disapprovingly but he didn't care. He had to let Vlamis know that he understood. That at least one person shared in her triumph over chaos.

After she left the stage, Francis sat back, quite worn out, and checked his watch. It was later than he thought. If he left at intermission, he would just have time to make it to the office to meet his copy deadline. He hardly listened to the duet from *Lakmé,* so busy was he writing in his notebook.

At the typewriter in the city room, sparsely populated at this hour, he wrote quickly. The words came easily; he made few changes. When he took out the last sheet, he scanned it, then went to the computer room. As he waited for a typesetting console, a tiny memory jarred loose in his mind—a bit of old myth recalled from Bulfinch. King Midas had been asked to judge a song contest between Pan and Apollo. He had listened, then picked the wrong singer—cloven-hoofed Pan instead of bright Apollo, vulgarity instead of art. Francis marveled briefly at the way his mind threw up just the appropriate memory.

Heading for a vacant seat, Francis reflected that the pages in his hand summed everything he now understood about music. He could not have written them a few years ago. Before meeting Charles. Before—his heart gave a little twist—losing Charles. The review constituted an artistic credo fashioned over a lifetime.

Back at his desk in the city room, Francis thought of the Midas myth again. Apollo, furious at not being awarded the palm, had caused the old judge's ears to grow long as a donkey's. Francis touched his own ear. It seemed a very just punishment for a mistaken verdict. How apt those old stories were!

He had trouble getting to sleep that night. His mind was overactive. He got up and took a pill but it didn't help. About two o'clock, the empty space next to him suddenly took on the shape of Charles Inverness. It was mysterious, really. He was almost convinced he could reach out and run his hand along the gully of Charles' chest, the flat pasted decals of his nipples, the blue star on his arm (a souvenir of Macao). He might even move closer and cradle that heavy body in his arms, tracing the contours and elongations of the flesh. He fought against this illusion, annoyed by it, but it persisted until his mind, in a sudden flip-flop, brought up the image of Vlamis, tall and frosty in her white gown. At the same time, the Bellini aria filled his ears and he relived its rescue from disaster. For some reason this calmed him, and after a few minutes, Charles' phantom evaporated, as if annoyed at the competition.

He was still groggy from the sleeping pill when he picked up the paper from the doorsill next morning. He found his review quickly. It was headed "Champion Divas Slug It Out in Songfest." A stupid sentence, he thought, but there was no way to control the headline writers.

He read the review while waiting for the coffee to boil. Several times a warning light went on in his head and he told himself he had gotten a little carried away. In the morning grayness, the words seemed rather... personal. Why had he mentioned things like pain and adversity and loneliness? What did they have to do with music? Well, there was no help for it. It was too late to rewrite. If some of the other critics had a few snickers over breakfast—Francis Burns and his artistic credo!—well, that was their privilege. None of them had the courage to expose their deepest selves in print. That was some consolation.

The phone call came while he was shaving. There was nothing unusual about a phone call at ten on Saturday morning, but for some reason his stomach tightened at the sound. As he picked up the receiver, he fought off a slight tingle of dread.

It was his boss, Emile Thorborg, head of the music staff. He sounded tired. He was in the office. Could Francis come down?

"This morning?" Francis asked.

"If you don't mind." As Francis hung up, he noticed that the receiver was moist with sweat from his palm.

Emile greeted him pleasantly in his paper-strewn office and they chatted for a while. Emile, who had been born in the midwest of Swedish parentage, had round eyes of cornflower blue that reminded Francis of pictures of the planet earth taken from outer space. At last Emile inquired lightly where Francis had sat last night. When Francis replied that he had sat in the twelfth row as usual, Emile drummed on his blotter and said, "I thought they might have put you in a dead spot."

Francis was surprised at this but said nothing.

"Your reviews have changed recently, Francis." Emile fixed him with his earth-blue stare and smiled.

"How do you mean?"

"It's hard to put my finger on it exactly. But you seem to be in a minority about last night."

Francis looked at the pile of press-clips Emile was pushing across the desk. He could see headlines full of praise for Luigini.

"What's the difference?"

"No difference," Emile replied. "We want you to say what you believe. Only... everyone agreed that Vlamis was in awful voice last night. You wrote a rave."

Francis stared at Emile, taking in details he had never noticed before. The skin on his boss's face was dry and yellow, his neck deeply seamed. "Are you telling me I don't hear right?" He leaned across the desk. "That there's something wrong with the way I hear?"

"No... no," Emile twisted away. "There's nothing wrong with your hearing. It's just a question of... well, whether you hear the way other people do."

Francis laughed harshly. "My hearing is probably a great deal better than other people's."

"Even your colleagues?"

Francis decided not to answer. Emile cleared his throat. "Mr. Gastein was there last night with his wife. You know she's on the board at the Met."

"I know she's on the board," Francis replied scathingly, thinking of all the ladies who dabbled in the arts because their husbands were important.

"They both disagreed with your... um, verdict. Quite strongly."

"Are you telling me I'm supposed to mold my opinion to Mr. Gastein's just because he publishes this newspaper?"

Emile's face seemed to sag slightly. "No. But Mr. Gastein did make a suggestion you might want to think about. Jim Blake is going to Buenos Aires for a year and that means we need someone to write the chess column. Since you did such a terrific job at Reykjavík a few years ago..."

Francis could hardly believe his ears as Emile went on, promising reinstatement on the music staff after a while. "... Office politics," Emile concluded, spreading his hands. "I think Mrs. Gastein wants us to hire a friend of her daughter's. Probably just for the summer." He paused and Francis noted that he looked grief-stricken.

Francis waited a moment, then stood up without speaking. He was afraid that if he did, Emile would hear a tremor in his voice. He didn't want that. Emile came around the desk and put out his hand, but Francis stepped back. He didn't want a consoling pat. He didn't want to be stroked. That would have been the last straw.

His last glimpse of Emile was as he stood sadly by his desk, looking like a man who had been thwarted of an act of kindness.

Francis hardly saw the other people on the way down to the street. His head was buzzing too loudly. He had been dismissed. There was no other word for it. Dismissed to make way for some musicology major from Vassar. And why? Because he had chosen the unpopular way, the road not taken by the mob. He had chosen art, true art, over vulgarity— Apollo instead of Pan. It had not been an easy choice. It had required strength, self-confidence. And now he would have to pay for it.

On the street, he found everything in sharp focus, as if his vision had suddenly cleared. He walked through Times Square like a visitor from outer space, seeing it clearly for the first time. Could this be his city? Could these grim people be his fellow-citizens? He noted the hideous signs of commerce, the junk in the shops, the pale blue smoke of death emitted by the cars. Amazing he had never seen it all before!

Passing a record shop, he caught sight of a stack of opera albums by Fiora Luigini. On one of the covers she was shown as Violetta, in the same blue gown she had worn last night. A wave of hatred swept through him as he turned his head away.

It was this amazing clearsightedness that revealed Charles Inverness to him. Charles was in a coffee shop at 53rd and Broadway, eating a sandwich. Francis sent his burning gaze through the window just as Charles took a big bite. He stopped walking. In another moment, he knew, Charles would look up and see him.

And that was how it happened. Charles spotted Francis, then nodded and held up a finger. He wanted Francis to wait. Francis stood on the pavement while Charles wolfed the rest of the sandwich. When he came through the revolving door into the sunshine, his face bright with pleasure, Francis had the feeling that no time had elapsed since they had last met, even though it was actually a year.

They hugged with enthusiasm, then fell into step, walking north. Francis had an intense feeling of homecoming. How many years had he and Charles spent strolling the streets like this? How many times had he caught glimpses of Charles' fine profile and majestic shoulders as they made their way through the crowds? How many times had he listened while Charles expressed doubt, fear, happiness about his career as a singer?

Now Charles was talking about a concert tour of New England he had just finished. But Francis found himself only half-listening. He had suddenly remembered the first tour he and Charles had made together—a junket through Mexico. He had gone along to play the accompaniments, to save money. In Guadalajara, after the final concert, they had celebrated by drinking margaritas on the terrace of a café, under a sky of great brilliance. The tropical night around them had been full of fragrance and lust. Francis had never felt so open, so happy, so full of the possibilities of life. He had felt as if he had come out of forty years' sleep into a world made especially for him. They had staggered back to the hotel, holding each other up, laughing like school boys, and made love until the sun came up.

"You seeing anybody these days?" Charles' voice was elaborately casual. It seemed to come from a great distance away.

Francis came out of his reverie with a start. What did Charles want to know? He turned to look at his companion. His face was clear, innocent. At the same time a knocking started in his chest.

"No," he said. Then, since that sounded inadequate, he added, "I'm living alone and liking it."

Charles nodded, as if that was what he wanted to hear. Then he told Francis about his own situation. But again Francis only half-listened. He knew that Charles was living alone, that the new romance—he couldn't quite recall the young man's name—hadn't worked out. But what was the message for him, really?

He had the feeling that something unpleasant was about to happen.

"... and so when things didn't pan out, I applied for a studio in Carnegie Hall. I was lucky because this old lady who'd lived there for a hundred years died and..."

Charles was still talking when they came to a stop in front of Francis' apartment house. Francis, facing Charles, could see the ankh symbol he had given him on their second anniversary. It was resting on a black tuft of chest hair.

"Well, here's the old place," Charles peered into the lobby. "Where's Hector?"

"Hector's gone. They put in an automatic elevator."

Charles nodded, then started on an anecdote about Hector. Francis let his gaze travel down Charles' solid form, noting the deep chest, the slim waist, the long legs. For an instant he imagined the secret places under the clothes and remembered the night in Guadalajara, when they had made love until dawn.

Charles had stopped talking and was waiting to be invited upstairs. He wanted to be friends again. Wanted...

Francis' mind was in a whirl. Was this the unpleasantness he had anticipated? And why should it be unpleasant?

Suddenly, unexplainably, he felt angry. "I can't ask you up right now, Charles." His voice, he noticed, was unsteady. The knocking in his chest had speeded up.

Charles studied him with big dark eyes. Francis could see reproach forming in their depths. In another moment, he was afraid, his anger would evaporate, his resistance would crumble. He would ask Charles inside.

And then Charles put his large square hand on Francis' shoulder and squeezed it hard. Francis felt the warmth flow through him. How familiar it was! How full of the past!

"What's the matter, Fran?" Charles' voice was husky. Francis was aware of the overpowering scent of Charles' cologne. He had started him on that cologne—how many years ago? The odor seemed full of an unbearable nostalgia.

His skin twitched under Charles' grip. He wanted to cry out. Nothing was the matter! Nothing! But under that, he knew, was a black hole of hurt and betrayal. Why had Charles called their relationship suffocating? Why had he demanded his freedom as if he were demanding air to breathe? Why had he taken up with that silly young man whose name escaped him—who had in turn deserted him?

But even as these thoughts chased through his mind, he knew they didn't matter. He had the answers. He had had them for years.

Yes, they were all alike—Charles and Fiora Luigini and Emile Thorborg. They all wanted to touch him, to press against his flesh, to make him respond. They all wanted to interfere with his peace, his privacy, to lure him into betrayal and loss. And he saw now that if he gave in to any one of them, he would have to give in to all of them.

The anger surged in him again, stronger now, and with a

toss of his shoulder he threw off Charles' hand. "Nothing is the matter, Charles," he said, quite steadily. "I can't ask you up because it isn't convenient."

The reproach was visible in Charles' eyes, but Francis took its measure without flinching. Then he wheeled around and walked toward the apartment. He was aware that Charles was still standing behind him, waiting for a sign.

But there would be no sign—not now, not ever. A new round of betrayal would not begin. Ahead of him, above him, all around him, a life of solitude and serenity waited. It would not be enough, he knew with a terrible finality, but it would see him through to the end of the song. To the last full measure. And that was the most important thing.

Upstairs, in the bright apartment, he chose his afternoon music with the greatest care. It was only later, much later, as he undressed for bed, that the tears came at last.

The Koan

NEAL VALENTI sat quietly, watching Anatole and the two guests crease their faces into the grimaces of social intercourse. The day was two-thirds over and he hadn't told Anatole about his decision. Two-thirds over and he hadn't had the courage. Yet, when he had gotten up this morning—rolled out of bed and switched off the blanket on his side—he had promised himself.

He should have mentioned it during breakfast. Anatole was always groggy before his sleeping pill wore off. Or on their way to the grocery after lunch. Anatole was usually sweeter around noon—direct sunshine seemed to soften him, like cheese. And now, in the evening, it was too late. Anatole was surrounded by friends and fortified by booze. He'd missed his chance.

"We were playing bridge on this glass-topped table," Anatole's voice took on a Texas twang after a few drinks, "and when I was dummy I groped this number next to me because I forgot about the glass top..."

Neal had heard that anecdote before. He really didn't want to hear it again. But he was too close to Anatole and Maury and Ted—just four feet across the sundeck—to blot them out entirely. Nevertheless, there were things he might do to neutralize the noises, float free. His Zen studies had taught him that he might remove himself from any unpleasantness simply by going through a little door in his mind marked Open Me.

"Of course, Neal doesn't approve." Anatole's voice, which

had thickened, reached him from a great distance. "He thinks you shouldn't mix bridge and sex."

Neal smiled, his cheeks turning into little round stones. "I don't even play bridge," he kept his voice pleasant.

"I tried to teach him," Anatole continued, "but he's awful at games. No talent."

It was true. He hated games, all of them—bridge and backgammon and Scrabble. His mind didn't work that way. Faced with boards and tiles and cards, he froze up. Worst of all was a horrid little game called Spill and Spell in which you threw dice with letters on them and made words before the sand ran out of an eggtimer (three minutes). When they played Spill and Spell he turned into a block of ice. But Anatole was crazy about games. He was never happier than when hunched over a board or puzzle or card table. He liked word games best of all.

"I never play bridge with anyone humpy," Maury, the older guest, remarked. He was tall and narrow-chested and wore two rings on each hand.

"The ladies at the bridge club adore him," said Ted, who was dark and handsome.

As the conversation continued, Neal wondered if he should go in the bedroom and do a few exercises. What a relief it would be! He glanced at Anatole. He was looking his best tonight, much younger than his forty-seven years. Of course, this was the kind of scene that agreed with Anatole. Sunday evening in the house at Fire Island. Guests and booze on hand. The day's crossword puzzle completed and Neal clobbered at Spill and Spell not once but three times.

Neal could feel the frustration, a dark shape with spiky points, mounting in his chest. If he didn't get away now, before dinner, he'd be stuck. He could feel Anatole's huge blue eyes on him—opalescent jewels set in a skin tanned to the color of flayed deerskin. Anatole knew what he was thinking, had read his unsettled glance, his silence. Had read the signs and disapproved. He wanted Neal to stay. Stay and help make it a party.

Maury had started a long story about a houseboy. One of his neighbors had taken in a young man at the beginning of the summer. But instead of staying home and doing the chores, as promised, the houseboy had roamed the island with a pair of handcuffs dangling from his belt. He was fond of forcible restraint. Most mornings his employer had to scour the bushes and release the young man from captivity.

Anatole was nodding as he listened, as if he had known the houseboy story would come to a bad end. Anatole, Neal knew, prided himself on being realistic. He was never surprised by odd or mean behavior. If he heard some news of human weakness or immorality he would shrug and say, "Well of course, what did you expect?"

But Maury's tale had made Neal a little uneasy. There was a certain resemblance between the houseboy's situation and his own. A resemblance he didn't care to be reminded of.

He had let Anatole pick him up at tea dance four months ago, in early June. He had let himself be picked up because he had no place to spend the night. And after that first night he had accepted Anatole's casual offer of further hospitality. He knew he was swapping his body—it was a small, young body with knobby muscles and sallow skin—for bed and board. He had rationalized this to himself in various ways, but not with complete success. He hadn't really intended to stay more than a few days, a week at most. He had his work in the city—he painted apartments at nonunion rates—but he had let himself be seduced. Seduced not only by Anatole's hospitality, but by the splendor of sea and sky, the days that unfurled like blue banners, the sand dunes that reminded him of ruined Arab forts. Anatole's house was a quiet place on the last walk, far from the harbor and its bars and restaurants. After a few days it began to seem very cozy. Almost like home, in fact.

But it wasn't only the house and the scenery that had lured him to remain. It was also Anatole. Under the gameplayer and the skeptic was someone else, someone quite different. This person came out mostly at bedtime, when they were snuggled under the electric blanket (Anatole suffered from chronic chilliness even in July). Then Anatole would become sweet and silly and endearing, holding Neal close as he told him about his childhood in Waco, about his stern parents, about being seduced by a high-school jock when he was thirteen. At these times his voice would lose its flat, uninflected tone and become breathy with affection. After a few nights of this, Neal decided that Anatole, the real Anatole, was only visible after dark. He came out with the planets and the stars.

Anatole's final generosity—the one that had made Neal extend his stay indefinitely—had come at the end of the first week. Anatole had to go to the West Coast to visit a client. He might rent out his house for a huge sum, but instead he invited Neal to use the house himself. The offer—Anatole hardly knew him then, really—had taken Neal's breath away. And then he understood that Anatole, despite his imperturbable manner, was lonely. From that had come the final rationalization—he was doing Anatole a favor by staying on.

Maury had embarked on another story, this one about nudity on the beach. Neal stood up. "I'm going inside," he announced.

Anatole glared at him. "You can't meditate now, we're going to have dinner." His long thin face was made longer by disapproval.

"I've got time."

"Oh have a drink and forget all this meditation business," Maury said. His voice was humid. If you squeezed it, Neal thought, you'd get a pint of water.

"He doesn't drink," Anatole said piously. He swirled his martini and Neal thought he might get nasty. But he made only a dry remark about people who couldn't be sociable.

As Neal closed the door to the bedroom and sank to the floor, sitting zazen in perfect balance, he blotted out the images of the cocktail hour and began to concentrate on his breathing. But it didn't come easily. His mind skittered around; his stomach was cold and tense.

Then, making an effort, he reached for the face of his Zen master. The roshi had a soft round visage and observed the world placidly through tortoise-shell frames. Neal tried to picture him in the garden of the monastery at the time of the giving of the koan. The roshi spoke only when absolutely necessary. In every way he was just the opposite of Anatole.

The thought was disturbing. In a flash, the scene outside popped into his mind. Anatole was probably still complaining about him. The others would be nodding and smiling, their eyes bright with disapproval and lust. The scene had no message for him—none at all, but there it was, occupying his mind, pushing everything else aside.

Why hadn't he told Anatole about his decision? It could have been done swiftly, neatly.

I've got to be getting back, Anatole. I'm sick of your games, bored with your two-tiered personality. It was okay for a while, but that's over now...

But he had not. Had not... been able to. Something had prevented him. What?

His mind moved suddenly and he decided to skip the preliminaries of breathing. He would direct his thoughts toward the koan. But of course, that was all wrong. You weren't supposed to direct your thoughts at all. No mapped or charted route took you to Awareness. Awareness wasn't a place at the end of the road, for God's sake. Nor was Awareness not thinking about Anatole. Awareness wasn't here or there, nor was it—for that matter—not here or not there. It simply was. How many times had he tried to explain that to Anatole? Anatole could not understand. Or would not.

A gust of laughter pierced the room. The koan—quickly! But it wouldn't come. Instead, he saw the face of Father Bernard, his Latin teacher at the seminary outside Doylestown. On cue, the terrible cold returned, in spite of the fact that the room he was sitting in was quite warm. They had half-frozen the seminarians all winter—it was part of the sacrifice, part of the toughening-up to do God's work—but Neal had never been able to accept it. It was the cold, even more than the sadistic teachers like Father Bernard, that had convinced him he was not cut out to be a priest.

And then, unannounced, the words of the koan circled lazily out of nowhere and entered his mind, sending warm waves along the secret flues of his body. Instantly, miraculously, he felt his midriff heating up, the cold of the seminary forgotten.

The path has no doors, yet they are marked no entrance and no exit.

The koan floated around, meaningless yet reassuring, in the pale sunshine of his belly.

The path has no doors, yet they are marked...

How inviting the words were! He leaned against them, feeling his weight make them yield slightly. In another moment they opened up and he saw that they led to a maze. He put his foot on the first word, treading carefully. In another moment he was inside the maze, the words crinkling deliciously underfoot. How warm he felt! His body was a vessel filled with sunshine. Snaillike, round and round, he entered the maze. Then he discovered, to his surprise, that the center, the very heart of the maze, contained a flower. A rose.

The bedroom door flung open. It was Anatole. Peering over his shoulder were Ted and Maury.

"We've come to see what you actually do," Anatole said, his voice flat but imperious.

"I bet he's playing with himself," Maury cackled, "he's so selfish."

He wrenched away from the rose at the heart of the maze. They were all drunk. Maury was swaying. The rings on each hand glittered in the gloom.

"Yes, we want a really good explanation," Anatole said. He moved to the bed and sat down. "I must get this bedspread cleaned," he remarked.

Neal unfolded his legs and stood up. Anatole's long face was prim with false interest. "We're waiting," Anatole said, then looked up at him and cleared his throat ostentatiously.

And then, oddly, Neal saw Anatole's face as a kind of maze, a place of curves and turnings, where he had hoped to find a center. Now, looking at Anatole as he sat on the edge of the bed, he understood that the quest had been in vain. Whenever he had reached for the center, thought he could touch the flower at the heart of the maze, it had eluded him. It was a search for something that was never there. And now the time had come to give up. To stop looking. He took a deep breath. The words, when they came out, seemed to have only the most distant connection with him.

"I've been meaning to tell you all day. I'm going back to town first thing in the morning."

Anatole regarded him levelly. "Just like that."

"Just like that." Neal was aware of heavy breathing in the silent room. "I'll see you in the city," he said.

Anatole swirled his drink. "No you won't."

Neal shrugged. He could think of nothing to say. Or could he? Several sentences took shape in his mind, sentences that might unlock the impasse, but what was the use?

Then, in spite of his resolve, he put out his hand and rested it on Anatole's shoulder. At the contact, he felt Anatole's skin quiver, like a horse's flank when a fly lands. A reflex, no more. But it brought back all their nights under the electric blanket when Anatole had whispered stories about church socials and berrypicking and shopping trips to Dallas, about his arrival in New York two decades ago as a slender smooth-faced young man, about his hope that Neal would stick around a while longer. All that seemed to transmit itself through the thin bones, spreading through Neal's arm and body in familiar waves. And then he registered the urge to press further, into the very core of Anatole's personality, into the heart of the maze, and he thought for one precious moment that he could, that it needed only one last bit of love and trust . . .

"Take your cottonpickin' hands off me," Anatole said.

He moved away. Anatole stood up. "You can leave whenever you want," he said. "Nobody's stopping you."

Neal wasn't sure who left the room first—he was confused and it had gotten quite dark—but he saw Anatole shake his head and blink rapidly at the door and then he was alone. For once Maury and Ted hadn't said anything. Maybe the scene had embarrassed them. Well, that didn't matter either. Nothing mattered except that he had gotten his marching orders. It was time to pack up.

As he filled his suitcase, he heard voices coming from the deck. The usual chatter about sex, although he could not identify Anatole's voice. Folding his clothes, Neal wondered what he should do next. The last ferry for the mainland had already left. He knew Anatole would probably not mind if he spent the night. Still, he didn't want to ask the favor. Not now.

When his small wardrobe was neatly stowed away in the zipper case, he gave a last look around at the walls of knotty pine, the seashells on the bureau, the vast bed whose counterpane undulated with a wave pattern. It certainly seemed like home. But it was not. Had never been—quite.

He would have to pass through the group on the front deck in order to leave. He wished he didn't have to, but there was no help for it.

"I'll be back in the morning for my things," he said. Anatole was sitting quietly in a chair in the far corner of the deck.

"Well sure." Anatole's voice was high, almost lilting. Neal had never heard that tone before. He moved to the edge of the deck. "You can spend the night if you want." It was Anatole again, speaking with an effort. Neal couldn't make out his expression.

"Thanks, I'll stay with Carlos."

He thought he heard a snicker from Maury but he wasn't sure. He stepped to the walk that led out to the wooden boulevard. Behind him he heard silence, then rapid footsteps. He turned. It was Anatole.

"If I've done something to offend you, I'm sorry." Anatole stood a few feet away, picking at a leaf. What could he say?

That he was tired of backgammon and bridge and Spill and Spell?

"You haven't offended me."

"I wish you'd stay." Anatole's voice went even higher, then cracked. "I really do." Neal was overcome with embarrassment. He had never heard Anatole plead for anything. This loss of control seemed out of place—something that belonged to the repertory of night and the bedroom.

"I'll see you in the morning," he murmured before hurrying off. He looked back only once. Anatole was still standing in front of the house, his head bowed, a slim figure in blue denims.

Carlos Ibarra lived two walks away in a house called Casa Blanca. He showed no surprise when Neal walked in the front door. He was a heavy man with a moist air, as if he sweated secretly, and had two large moles on his clavicle. He was from Bogotá—a rich expatriate.

Seeing Carlos' flashy and expensive furniture, just the opposite of Anatole's, and his quickly proprietary attitude, Neal had a moment of doubt. Perhaps it would be better to take his chances at the bar. But Carlos, sensing his hesitation, reassured him. "No one going to bother you in there," he waved at one of the bedrooms. "You sleep like an *angelito*." He patted his hands together and smiled.

It was easy talking to Carlos, although it took some time to find out why. Then Neal realized that Carlos dealt only with strong emotions. His feelings were his only interest. Listening to the juicy phrases, soaking in the passions, which bloomed in the air like exotic flowers. Neal was aware that his whole body was relaxing. He had forgotten how easy, how refreshing it was to talk about things like love and anger and hate. Things didn't have to be as complicated as they were in Anatole's house.

As Carlos went into detail about one of his many love affairs, Neal wondered if it was some lack of his own that had kept him with Anatole all summer. But he dismissed the thought after a while. If that were so, why would he feel so relieved now? Why would he have left Anatole for good?

But his host's prediction that he wouldn't be bothered during the night didn't turn out to be true. Toward morning, Neal was wakened by soft footsteps. He could just make out a large figure with furry shoulders standing over him and making moist sounds. In another moment, the figure was stretched out beside him, running spongy fingers over his chest, crooning softly. He was too inert to move and soon a pair of lips had fastened onto his sex, lips that were expert and selfless. Still drugged with sleep he responded. Everything seemed to move outward, as if this weren't really happening, and he had a brief, strangled climax. "Nice," Carlos murmured in the dark. In another moment he was gone and Neal went back to sleep.

In the morning, Carlos served coffee with a patronizing air and didn't refer to the events of the night before. "If you like, you stay with me," he said, "forget all that shit." He waved a hand in the direction of Anatole's house. "I got nobody to love right now." He didn't seem to expect an answer.

Neal watched him pour his coffee, light with milk, over a bowl of cornflakes. It seemed an unappetizing combination but Carlos spooned it with gusto. Neal's question tumbled out almost without his willing it. "Do you like to play cards?"

"Me cards? You crazy?" Carlos tapped himself on his chest—he was wearing a tank-top of shiny red acetate—and laughed. "I doan have time for that."

Neal cleared the table while Carlos talked some more. He found himself listening with less attention than the night before, but still he enjoyed the excitement in Carlos' voice, the clear laughter with which he related his stories. When he finished the dishes, Carlos suggested they go to the beach. Without thinking, Neal looked around for the Scrabble set— Anatole never went to the beach without it—but then caught himself. It wouldn't be necessary today.

At the beach, Carlos was even more expansive. Unlike

Anatole, he knew almost everyone in sight. As these people came over and were introduced, Neal realized he was being shown off as a trophy. Though this had happened to him before, it always made him uneasy. It seemed a violation of his self-respect, somehow. Still, it was clear that Carlos was full of goodwill, was only trying to be friendly, so he suppressed his distaste. Toward noon, feeling quite drained by all the small talk, Neal decided to go back to the house. He would sit zazen for a while. He didn't tell this to Carlos—merely said he had an errand to do—but Carlos jumped up and said he would come along.

When they reached the house, Carlos followed Neal into the bedroom. When he found out that Neal had come back in order to meditate, his eyes grew round with interest. "I watch, okay?" he asked.

Somewhat irritably, Neal explained that solitude was necessary. Carlos didn't understand this at first—in fact, it took some insistence on Neal's part to persuade him to leave, and then it was only because Neal had promised to give him some lessons in Zen later in the day.

As Neal settled to the floor, facing the wall, he reflected that Carlos, unlike Anatole, was sociable by day and secretive by night. Then he noticed that Carlos' scent, which was a blend of cucumber soap and musk oil, lingered in the room. This annoyed him unreasonably, and he had to force himself to concentrate on his breathing for a long time before he could forget it. At last his mind began to drift and the familiar warmth settled in his belly. Soon the roshi appeared, looking beatific behind his moon frames. The roshi's presence expanded and Neal found himself in the garden behind the monastery, receiving the koan. The syllables flowed over him again.

The path has no doors, yet they are marked no entrance and no exit.

The familiar paradox soothed him tremendously. It seemed a delicious antidote to everything that had happened today. The koan repeated itself several times more. Then, very faintly, Neal heard a click and he saw that a space had opened in his head, a space he had never known was there. Stepping into it, he found himself in the midst of a yellow aura shaped rather like a rose. In the center of this aura, dressed in blue denims, was Anatole. He felt a faint tug of resistance—he really didn't want to see Anatole right now—but he soon realized that this was not the Anatole he knew so well but a different person altogether, someone quite in harmony with his new, unearthly surroundings.

"Hi," the new Anatole said, in a warm and friendly way. His blue eyes were endlessly deep. "Hi," Neal replied.

Then Anatole reached in his pocket and took out an electronic calculator. He pushed some of the buttons and said, "I just know I can figure this out." Neal waited while Anatole pushed the buttons some more, in all kinds of combinations, and then at last Anatole smiled and nodded. "See," he said, holding up the calculator, "when you're out, you can't get in. And when you're in, you can't get out." At that, he dropped the calculator and his blue eyes filled with tears.

When Neal came out of the trance, he found that his eyes were wet but that his body was receiving enormous energy. In fact, he was filled with an explosive force that seemed to pulse through him until it reached the top of his skull. He stood, almost levitated, up and looked around with a sharpness of vision he had not experienced in years. Every ornament, every picture and chair, seemed to throb with life. For an instant he had the impression that these objects were about to hurtle toward him and he ducked. Then, shielding his face, he walked out of the house.

On his way to Anatole's, he was filled with jubilation. Each step on the boardwalk seemed terribly significant, as if his path were heralded with tongues of fire. The few people who passed looked at him curiously but he paid no attention.

The little cottage on the last walk appeared empty, but he knew this was deceptive. Anatole was in an easy chair with a huge dictionary open on his lap. Neal walked to the center of the room and stood breathlessly. Anatole did not look up, but this did not surprise him.

"Do you know that *quod* and *za* are perfectly good words?" Anatole's voice was flat and dry, but at the same time comforting.

"No, I didn't."

"Well, they are."

Neal was aware of the energy jostling him from all sides. "You know, Anatole," he said, "Zen is a kind of puzzle too."

Anatole shrugged. "Of course. What did you expect?" He looked up and now Neal could see that he was much paler, as if he had faded last night while he slept alone.

"I missed you," Neal said, taking a step closer. "Carlos is an idiot."

Anatole nodded, as if he had expected this information too. Then he rose, closing the dictionary, and went to the closet where he kept all his games. "What'll it be?" he asked.

As Neal hesitated, it came to him that if Anatole was just the opposite of his Zen teacher, then these games were just the opposite of meditation, and Fire Island was the opposite of both the seminary where he had failed to become a priest and the monastery where he had failed to attain Enlightenment. And then a flare went off in his mind and he saw with trembling clarity that the koan had been devised to reveal to him that the opposite of everything in the world was also true.

Anatole was waiting by the closet. His eyes were huge and troubled.

"Spill and Spell," Neal said at last. "I always hated that the most."

"I know," Anatole said. But, surprisingly, he made no further move. "Maybe," he said, "you'd rather talk."

But Neal shook his head sweetly. "No. Let's play."

The Bad Penny

IT WAS TURNING into one of those terrible family dinners. Nicky wondered where it had gone wrong, then decided it had gone wrong a hundred years ago, before any of them had met. They might even have been on a collision course when Venus sideswiped earth, which Velikovsky said was about 2000 B.C. The Red Sea had parted, Thera had blown up, and he and Mildred had begun to clash. Of course, Herbert, her husband and his brother-in-law, didn't help. Everything Herbert said was idiotic. Instant boredom poured from his mouth. He'd gotten very red in the face in the last few years, Nicky noticed, as if a low fire were burning in his gut. His alcohol ingestion, obviously the fuel of the fire, had increased too, though nowadays he tried to toss down the drinks when his wife wasn't looking.

Tonight that was when Mildred went to the ladies' room. Herbert jumped up, hurried to the restaurant bar, and put away two doubles while Nicky and Blair watched. He came back to the table, the flames scorching his forehead, and beamed at them. His cheeks bunched into little balls. "I'm a bad penny too," he remarked jovially, looking at Nicky. Then he sat down, searing them with his breath.

Nicky went cold all over. "What did you say?"

Herbert laughed again, but his glance flickered nervously toward Blair. "I mean *I'm* a bad penny."

Too late. Nicky knew what he meant. His head got light and he had the sensation of soaring. He, the good boy of the family, the one who always got A's, kept his room neat, graduated with honors, succeeded in business... he was in a class with Herbert! That's what they all thought! Two bad pennies!

He glared at Herbert, who was now looking at him with alarm. There was no question about Herbert's being a black sheep—a compulsive gambler, kiting checks at Harrah's, one step ahead of the sheriff at times. He and Mildred had been married for twenty years and had failed every marital test but one—they had produced two fine boys of college age. But that was enough. They were God's anointed, the elect of the earth.

Nicky passed his hand across his forehead. Families—how he hated them!

Blair, of course, had read his mind. "We're all bad pennies one way or another," he said helpfully. No one replied. Blair started a story about the time his father had taken him and his brothers to the town jail and locked them up, just to scare them out of any future misdeeds. But Nicky didn't listen. He'd just had a vision of his sister's family sitting around their dining room in San Bernardino, after having finished a meal on the Haviland china which she had inherited from mother. As they wiped their lips on the damask napkins—also inherited—they said nasty things about him and Blair. "Which one is the husband and which one is the wife?" (Slap, nudge, guffaw.) "Sure he's got a lotta money, who's he gonna spend it on, runaway boys?" (Slap, wink, giggle.) It was maddening.

Blair had finished his jail story and was waiting for a reaction. But Nicky refused to look up. He'd just decided, with a passion that surprised him, that he would follow through on his plan. He wouldn't chicken out—not out of family loyalty or good nature or fear. If he was a bad penny, by God, he'd show them what a bad penny could do.

The idea had come to him last week while shaving. As he scraped his cheeks and sculptured the ends of his brown mustache—still only lightly tinged with gray—he had thought about the impending visit of Mildred and Herbert, an annual affair. It would be horrible, as usual. Mildred really disapproved of him and Blair. She would cover this up with too much praise—praise of the pictures and furniture in their house overlooking the Bay, praise of their cooking, their friends, their careers. She would waltz around the house, exclaiming over this and that, her long narrow face alight with goodwill. Of course, she would avoid going in the bedroom, or remarking on its handsome platform bed. The bedroom, everybody knew, was out of bounds. The trouble was that she really did want to approve of them, did want to include them in her family embrace. "I'm the matriarch of the family now," she had announced when mother died a few years ago. And Nicky had sensed the pride and pleasure that position gave her. But for all her effort, she couldn't quite manage to approve of them. Something always stopped her. As she struggled against her revulsion, the praise poured out—squeals, cries, alarums of praise. It was exhausting. After they left he would go to bed and sleep for twelve hours.

Now, as he shaved, Nicky thought that it might be easier if Mildred simply expressed her outrage. But that, he sighed, was not the way things were done in his family. Appearances had to be maintained, nice things had to be said. Nobody told the truth about anything—it was a family tradition.

The idea hit him as he was slapping some Aramis on his cheeks. He gasped at the beauty of it. They should dig up Dranie! He stared at his reflection, noting that his cheeks were still firm but that his chin was showing signs of sag. Why hadn't he thought of that before? Digging up Dranie would be—he winced slightly at the paradox—a way of burying the past.

Dranie was their mother's mother. She had been given an elaborate Protestant burial in a cemetery in Westchester, back east. However, her husband, their maternal grandfather, lay in state in a Jewish cemetery in Queens, with a headstone engraved in Hebrew. The two, united in life, had been parted in death. The poor old lady had been lying in the wrong place for a quarter century!

Nicky giggled as he got dressed, wondering what would be involved in digging up a corpse and moving it fifty miles away. Would religious services be required for reburial? But under his giggles were goosebumps. His mother, he knew, would be appalled by such goings-on. Although she'd been raised as a Jew, she had turned her children over to the Episcopalians with as much determination as she had had her mother buried in an Episcopalian cemetery. She had always refused to discuss her conversion, dismissing it with statements like, "I don't identify with those people," or "Christ is my redeemer too." Undoing her decision now would be, Nicky realized, a kind of heresy.

He thought about the matter on and off during the day—he operated his own travel agency on lower Market Street. Of course, he hadn't discussed it with Blair yet, and Blair might advise him, as usual, to forget the past. But this time, he felt, that would be bad advice. There was something so right—so inexorably right—about the whole idea.

To his surprise, Blair didn't raise any objections. "I think that's a wonderful idea," he said that evening. "Dig her up and give her a Jewish burial." His eyes gleamed. "Do we all get to wear yarmulkes?"

Nicky grinned. Blair, an Anglo-Saxon from the midwest, adored minorities. "Yarmulkes, phylacteries, shawls, the whole bit," he replied.

"Marvelous," Blair glowed. He laid aside the student papers he'd been correcting. "What about Mildred?"

Nicky paused. He'd completely forgotten about Mildred. "She won't mind," he said vaguely.

"You better watch out, you'll have another one of your awful quarrels. You know how she feels about all that Jewish business."

It was true. Mildred never told people her mother had been Jewish, just as she never told anyone her brother was queer. "Maybe I don't need her. Maybe I can just do it and tell her afterward."

Blair made a face. "Fat chance."

Nicky checked his watch. Six-thirty. Too late to make a call back east. "First thing tomorrow I'm gonna call the cemetery and find out what's involved." he said.

Next morning while Blair was fixing breakfast, Nicky got the information operator in area 914. When he gave her the name of the cemetery, she checked her book and asked him if he wanted the mausoleum or the crematorium. The request gave him a creepy feeling. He chose the mausoleum.

A woman answered, "Cedarcliff."

For a moment Nicky was confused. Then he mumbled, "I'd like to speak to somebody about digging somebody up."

There was a pause at the other end. "You mean a disinterment." The woman's tone was reproving.

"Yeah, a disinterment." The word had a nice clean ring to it.

"Are you a funeral director?"

"Me? No."

Another pause while the woman repeated his request to someone. A smooth masculine voice came on.

"Can I help you?"

"Yes. I want to see about having someone disinterred and buried somewhere else. My grandmother."

"I see." The voice was warm and juicy. "You want to have grandmother buried with us."

"No, no. She's already there. I want her buried with her husband."

"I see. You want grandfather buried with us."

"No, no. He's in Queens. I want them together."

"Here."

"No. There."

Nicky heard a sigh. "You mean you're taking grandmother up?"

He wished the man wouldn't make it sound as if she were his grandmother too, but he only said, "Yeah, taking grandmother up."

"Well." The man's voice was suddenly cold and business-like. "That can be quite a problem. When was she buried?"

Nicky named the year.

"That was a long time ago. Who owns the plot?"

"My mother and father bought it."

"You'll have to get their permission to dig grandmother up."

"They're in it."

"What?"

"The plot. They're in it. They're dead."

"Well who owns it now?"

The man's patience was clearly running out. Nicky explained that he was the surviving male heir and executor of the estate and now lived in San Francisco. The man, who identified himself as a salesman (what was he selling—earth, death, the life to come?), advised him he'd need releases from all the direct descendants. He also said the disinterment would cost $300 unless the casket was in an underground vault, in which case it would be $200 extra. The conversation ended.

Feeling somewhat deflated, Nicky went back to the kitchen and repeated it all to Blair.

"I knew it," Blair said, "you'll have to have Mildred's consent."

Nicky felt his resolve weakening. There would be a fuss. Mildred would see no point in digging up Dranie and turning her into a posthumous Jew, overlooking the fact that she'd been one most of her life.

"Maybe I can talk her into it," Nicky said. Blair laughed ironically. He was right, Nicky thought. Mildred would see the whole thing as another gay fantasy, on the order of dressing up in drag. Nothing to do with the realities of family life, which included getting her boys into good schools and keeping Herbert out of jail.

With a depressing sense that the project was silly and trivial, Nicky stopped thinking about it for the rest of the week.

Until tonight, in the restaurant at Fisherman's Wharf.

What in the name of God was Mildred doing in the ladies' room? He had often noticed that she liked to take her time in there, but this was going on even longer than usual. He pictured her in front of the mirror, bullshitting with the other women, taking forever with her Maybelline. Suddenly he saw Mildred's sojourns in the ladies' as one more power play. She liked to keep people waiting. It proved she was important.

His plan for digging up Dranie expanded in his mind even more. It certainly didn't seem silly or trivial now. Quite the contrary—it seemed a fine and strong idea. It was up to him, the man of the family, to see that justice was done.

What in the name of God was she *doing* in there?

MILDRED APPLIED her Cover Girl with unsatisfactory results. New cracks—they were more like gullies—had opened up in the few hours since she'd left home. What a shame. She'd wanted to look her best for Nicky. If it weren't for her fine rosy skin and her recent trip to the hairdresser, she would look awful tonight. Frustration mounted in her, a dark shape surrounded by tears. Why had she put herself out like this? What did she get out of it?

Nicky had been his usual disagreeable self on the way in from the airport. Making no effort to rise to the occasion, not caring whether the evening was a success, whether they renewed their family feeling. He'd always been that way—sullen, a loner. "Nicky's sulling tonight," mother used to say, as Nicky, brooding over some imaginary slight, refused to speak to anybody. She heaved a sigh, thinking of her friends with brothers who liked to play golf. Her family was peculiar. In fact, she was the only normal one in it.

The woman next to her was saying how she loved San Francisco. Mildred smiled. How good it felt to smile! "We come here almost every year," she replied, "my brother lives here with his family." She watched the woman apply eyeliner with great care.

"That's nice," the woman said.

His family! If only it were true. What was the name of this one? She had forgotten it for some reason. The one before had been named Christopher. Or was it Crawford? Well, no doubt it would all come back to her when she joined them at the table.

She applied more liquid to the corners of her almond eyes. If only she were looking her best tonight! And then, surprisingly, more resentment welled up in her. Why should she care what Nicky, her baby brother, thought? What was the source of his power over her? She looked at herself sharply in the mirror, narrowing her eyes. He had had that power as long as she could remember. She shook her head, trying to clear it, realizing it was impossible to do so. Nicky was part of her, just as Herbert and the boys were part of her.

A sigh escaped her. She had just remembered Nicky's last visit to the hospital. A few hours before he was due, mother had sat up, suddenly imperious after weeks of passivity, and called for makeup. Makeup! She wanted to look her best for Nicky! And there was no denying her. Mildred had spent half an hour rouging her ashen cheeks, painting her gray lips, covering up the trail of cancer while mother urged her on. And she had understood mother's need, understood her hope that the decay might be camouflaged, the flesh restored, so that a man—a man she loved—might see her at her best. *Looking good!*

Nicky, of course, had no idea how hard they had worked to set the stage for him. He saw only a shriveled bundle with glittering eyes in an ill-fitting wig. But Mildred knew. Knew because she had been there, backstage where the illusion had been created.

And now she was doing the same thing! She sighed again and daubed on more Cover Girl.

"Have a lovely time in San Francisco," the woman next to her said, getting up. Mildred noted how the woman's blue eyes sparkled. She had always admired blue eyes.

"Thank you and you do the same." How nice people were. It often gave her a warm feeling to converse with strangers.

Nicky hadn't had it easy in life. Men who were that way never did. She'd have to remind herself of that tonight, if he started sulling. Make allowances.

No, it hadn't been easy for him. But it hadn't been easy for her either. She rested her hand on the dressing table and peered into the depths of her eyes. Nicky, in all his self-centeredness, had never really understood that her life was basically tragic.

Just last month she'd discovered that Herbert had pawned the diamond ring she had had made from mother's lavaliere. A flawless yellow stone, worth a fortune. Pawned it and gone to Las Vegas. Her stomach tightened now as she recalled the moment when she had spotted the fake stone on his finger. It didn't glow with a deep yellow light; it shone dully. "Herbert!" she had shrieked, knowing instantly from his sheepish look what he had done. She had burst into tears and locked herself in the bathroom.

Yes, her life had been tragic, even though it had started out so well.

She had gotten mother's diamond out of hock by using her own money, saved from her job. She hadn't given it back to Herbert. Oh no. She stashed the diamond in the safe deposit box, to which she alone had access. One day Thaddeus or Pierce would use it as an engagement ring for his bride. It would stay in the family. It would never go to some gambler or drug dealer.

She mustn't linger. They were all waiting. Herbert had probably been making trips to the bar. And Nicky was probably seething over her delay. Well, she couldn't help it. Let them wait. She wouldn't leave here until she was good and ready.

NICKY, seeing Blair jump up, looked around. It was Mildred, sweeping grandly across the dining room at last. He had to admit she looked good—tall, voluptuous, her hair bright, her skin glowing.

Blair pulled back her chair. "Such gallantry," she cooed, smiling at everyone.

"We thought you fell in," Nicky muttered. No one seemed to hear.

Mildred was giving off waves of goodwill. Nicky knew the signs. Family time. He and Blair, orphaned tots of forty-five and forty-two respectively, were about to be given some mother-love.

"It's so nice to be here," she said, "we've let too much time go by." She had a bad habit, Nicky recalled, of italicizing every other word.

"You have to come down and visit us real soon. You haven't seen our new pool, Blair."

Blair nodded. They started talking about southern versus northern California. Herbert had a lot of opinions on that subject.

Nicky turned and gestured for the waiter. If he didn't speed things up they'd be here all night.

Mildred changed her order three times. Each time she gave the waiter a brilliant smile, including him in some kind of conspiracy, so that he smiled too. As the waiter went off and they settled back, Nicky registered a twinge of remorse. He was really being churlish. Mildred was obviously making an effort. And she'd traveled all this way just to see him. He was out of sorts because of the bad penny crack. But his mother used to say two wrongs didn't make a right.

"What's the course you like to teach best?" Mildred had obviously given up on him and was concentrating on Blair.

"My favorite course?" Blair thought for a minute. "Gay literature, I guess."

Mildred jerked her head back and her eyelids fluttered rapidly. "How interesting!"

But Nicky had seen the jerk, read the flutter. He knew what they meant. Uneasiness, embarrassment, followed by cover-up. The Watergate cover-up was nothing compared to what went on in his family. Nixon had only sat on the truth for a few months, but they had been on top of it for generations. He felt his goodwill dissolving.

"What... um, authors, do you teach?" Mildred snapped her fingers. "Oscar Wilde, I bet!"

Nicky's stomach contracted. But Blair, bless him, nodded sweetly. "Also Gertrude Stein, E. M. Forster..." he reeled off a list of names. Mildred gave little encouraging nods.

Nicky had never heard Herbert utter the word "gay." The best he had ever been able to manage was "you fellows." He managed that now.

"All those famous writers, you fellows have a lot going for you," he said. He smiled at Nicky, clearly impressed with his own broad-mindedness.

Nicky closed his eyes briefly. He had the sudden impression that his family didn't use words, they used tampons—soft, absorbent packages to soak up the blood and guts. Then he saw quite clearly the course the evening would take. Three hours of polite nothings. Evasion. Fakery. *Tampons!*

"Mill."

She looked at him sharply, hearing something new in his voice. The table got quiet. "I have an idea."

She sat up and glanced at her husband. "Oh?" She covered her mouth with her hand—a nervous habit from adolescence when she was fearful of bad breath.

"I want to have Dranie dug up." The words fell on the tablecloth like little hard pellets.

Mildred cleared her throat softly. "What did you say?"

Nicky had the feeling that he was starting to roll down a long hill with no bottom. "I want to have Dranie dug up. Moved to another cemetery."

"What for?"

"I think she should be buried with her husband."

"Where's her husband?"

"In the Heavenly Gates Cemetery in Queens. I went out there just before I left the east. I told you."

"Oh yes."

Herbert let out a strangled sound. "What's the difference

where they are?" He leered at them. "They aren't going to do anything together." He looked hopefully at Blair, who smiled a little.

"That's not the point," Nicky said coldly. "She's buried in a Protestant cemetery and he's buried in a Jewish one. They should be together."

Mildred took a deep breath. Her nostrils dilated. "Why do you have to bring this up tonight when we're having such a good time?"

The old cop-out, of course. It was never the right time in his family. It was always too early or too late, or someone was tired or not in the mood.

"This is as good a time as any. I've been thinking about it for quite a while. I've already cleared it with the cemetery."

Not true, of course. Amazing how easy it was to lie when he was with his family. At other times he avoided lies like a nest of snakes.

"You did that without consulting me?"

"I'm consulting you now."

She was angry now, he could see. Her eyes narrowed in the old familiar way, dark slits in her white face. Her nose seemed to compress with rage.

"No you're not consulting me. You're telling me what you're going to do."

"I'm the head of the family and I can do it if I want."

Not true also, but there was no stopping him. He would lie from now till the end of time if necessary.

"Now hold the phone!" Herbert slammed his hand on the tablecloth. The silverware jumped. He was getting angry too. Nicky had the impression that they were both bloating with rage, and that if he took his dinner fork and punctured them, the room would fill with a foul gas. "Nobody gives a darn where your grandparents are buried. You're just doing this to upset Millie." He turned toward his wife. "Honey, we're going to forget about all this. Hear that?" He looked at Nicky, who recalled—for the first time in years—that Herbert had commanded a PT boat in the Pacific during World

War II and had actually earned the respect of his men. "We're going to forget this. Right now." He spoke loudly and the people nearby looked around.

Mildred leaned toward him. "You are incredibly selfish," she hissed. Nicky looked furiously at Blair. Why hadn't he said anything? Why did he have to fight this battle alone? Mildred followed his gaze.

"What do you think, Blair? Don't you think it's a mistake to dig up these old things?"

Blair frowned. "Nicky... feels strongly about this," he murmured. He looked worriedly at Nicky, who glared back.

"We all do," Mildred said. Her voice was suddenly soothing. "And I think we should consider it. Carefully."

"But not rush off half-cocked," Herbert chimed in.

All of them turned and looked at him. He felt like a maddened dog at bay. He wiped his lips.

"We understand how you feel," Mildred said, "but will you please not ruin the party?"

Understand how you feel. But she didn't. None of them did. Suddenly, unaccountably, he felt his defiance dribbling down his leg. Did he understand himself? Did it really matter about Dranie—a fat old lady in a corset whom he hardly remembered? Was it worth all this trouble? All this hatred?

Herbert was loosing an avalanche of words. They flowed around the table in a glutinous mass, impossible to stop. About problems with his own sister, about children not getting along, about grandparents, about brothers. It was rambling and pointless, but everybody listened, relieved. Nicky felt exhaustion seep through him. How did they do it? How did they disarm him? He'd only been with them an hour and he felt like an old man. Herbert's words piled up, pinning them to their chairs.

No, it didn't really matter where Dranie was buried.

T<small>HE DRIVE UP TO</small> Pacific Heights from Fisherman's Wharf always terrified Mildred, though the ride down was worse. Going up now, she noticed that Blair was a terrible driver, tailgating, using brakes on the steep hill. Herbert, beside her in the back, was even more nervous. But he had a passion for driving, while her passion was merely for staying alive.

Blair was pointing out some of the mansions they passed, but it was too dark to see. Besides, she was getting a headache.

She looked at Nicky's profile in the front seat. How attractive her brother had become, though he certainly hadn't started out that way. He'd been one of the ugliest creatures in the world, with sallow skin and irregular features.

He didn't know how lucky he'd been. In all his self-pity, all his selfishness, he had never understood that. First, there was mother's endless devotion. Nicky had been her pet. It had often seemed to Mildred that Nicky had simply deprived her of a mother. Even after Nicky had made his famous avowal of his sexual habits, which had been in the worst possible taste, mother still favored him. Favored him even over her two young grandsons, which had annoyed Mildred no end. Sometimes she suspected that mother had actually approved of abnormality.

Then there was the question of brains. Nicky's report cards flashed before her eyes in the back seat now, glowing mysteriously with A's and 100s. How did he do it? She knew the answer to that. Reading all the time. He never had any friends, or any interest in sports. While she was out in her blue rompers batting the puck around in field hockey, he was home. Of course you knew the ruler of Venice was called the Doge if you sat home with a book all afternoon.

"We wish you'd change your mind."

It was Blair. He was really quite sweet. She couldn't imagine why she had forgotten his name.

"We'd love to, but Herbert has to be back early tomorrow."

Blair had made reservations for their trip to Alcatraz, but she had decided they would leave first thing in the morning. She'd made a success of the evening, but she simply didn't have the strength to keep them going another day. A shame, since they'd been looking forward to seeing Alcatraz.

"Well, see how you feel in the morning."

Blair again. Nicky sulling. Well, she knew how she'd feel in the morning. Tired. No question about *that*.

"Yes, we'll see," she murmured agreeably.

They were at the top of the hill now, thank heavens, still alive. She'd say goodnight the minute they got home.

"Look after Nicky, he's a weak reed." Mother's voice came back to her now, alarmingly distinct in the back of the car. They had been sitting on the couch just before mother went for her last trip to the hospital. "Promise you won't fight with him." Mother had put her wasted hand, once so strong and brown, on Mildred's sleeve and Mildred had smelled her tainted breath and stifled the urge to draw back. "I will," she had said firmly, and she meant it. She believed in promises like that—the promises between women that kept families together, kept the generations from blowing apart. It was that promise that brought her to San Francisco every year even though she didn't want to, even though she knew her family feelings were unreciprocated by Nicky.

"Home at last!" Blair said happily.

"Jiggity-jog," Nick said, his first words since they left the restaurant.

"Yes," she said, putting cheer in her voice. "The house looks wonderful. I'm so glad you bought it."

Of course, mother couldn't have foreseen this nonsense about Dranie when she made her promise not to fight with Nicky. She wouldn't have liked it one bit. Mother had wanted them to be free of all that Jewish nonsense, free of the prejudice that had undoubtedly marred her own childhood, though she never cared to talk about it. That's why she had sent them to St. Paul's, made sure they attended Sunday school, got confirmed, joined the young people's. So they'd be just like everybody else.

Why did Nicky insist on it, bringing it up when there was no need? He had even told her once that according to Hebrew law they were Jewish because they had a Jewish mother.

What nonsense. She was no more Jewish than she was Chinese. And the same went for the boys. She certainly hadn't told them about their grandmother's religious background. It was none of their business. And she'd warned Nicky against shooting off his mouth in front of them.

Maybe... the thought struck her as quite startling and she sat up straight... maybe Nicky was one of those people who enjoyed hurting themselves. Insisting on a Jewish identity was a way Nicky had of abusing himself. It was connected to his sex urge, though she certainly didn't want to pursue that line of thought too far.

They were in the garage. She fumbled around for the door handle until Herbert turned it for her. Then somebody turned on the garage light and she could see. They still had to go up a long flight of outside steps, though, which she dreaded.

She began pulling herself up, step by step, Herbert's hand under her elbow. Nicky and Blair bounded up the stairs, she noticed, as if they were sixteen years old. It was astonishing. Then she stopped, catching her breath. Maybe they *were* sixteen years old. Maybe they had never grown up, even though they were both middle-aged men.

"Come on, honey," Herbert said, "just a little bit more and then you can lie down."

She watched Nicky and Blair disappear inside. The house suddenly seemed bleak, untenanted. Nicky, with all his rooting around in the past, his interminable search for identity, had missed the point. The point was children, family, love. You gain your life by losing it. The old truths were best after all.

There! She had made it to the top. She moved into the house cautiously, as if it might be full of trapdoors. Just one night, she thought, and then she'd be home.

A unifying warmth poured through her. She had kept her promise in spite of everything. In spite of Nicky's selfishness, perversity, sulling. She could hear mother's approval even now—approval that bounced and echoed around the childless house with its perfect, polished furniture.

NICKY AVOIDED speaking to Blair as they got ready for bed. He answered Blair's questions with a grunt. He simply didn't want to go over the evening—not yet.

And, worst of all, Mildred and Herbert were right down the hall. The house didn't even seem his anymore. Unreasonably, he thought of it as his childhood home, which had also been occupied by a strange and frightening couple—his parents.

He got into his side of the bed and pulled all the blankets over him with a savage gesture. Blair had dropped out of the conversation tonight just when he needed him. Herbert had stood by Mildred, but Blair had chickened out. He looked at him now, putting on his mini-pajamas with short sleeves and legs. All of Blair's trim cuteness seemed distinctly unappealing this evening. He couldn't rely on Blair either. He wrapped the blankets tightly around him. Let Blair freeze his ass off.

"You always let her get to you," Blair said, coming toward the bed. Nicky didn't reply. "You're bad for each other."

Nicky thought about Blair's endorsement, just the week before. Words of accusation formed on his lips, but he said nothing. Blair lay down. Nicky grabbed the covers more tightly. They lay still for a moment. Then Blair said, "If you don't let go the goddam blankets I'm going to sleep in the living room." Nicky didn't move. Blair raised himself on one elbow. "What the fuck is the matter with you?"

Nicky made a face and released the blankets. Blair settled himself under them and turned off the light. After a while, Nicky felt Blair shifting towards him. He knew the signs. Blair would translate their estrangement into a little cuddling. He shifted further away.

Then he had a sudden picture in his mind. "Do you think they're going to have sex in there?" he asked aloud, his voice full of horror.

"Of course not."

"Why not?"

"They only do it Saturday night after a couple of drinks."

"Herbert's been drinking ever since he got off the plane."

Blair made a disgusted noise. "Will you cut it out, please?"

Nicky subsided, and the image vanished magically from his mind. God, he was exhausted. Thank goodness, they'd decided to leave first thing in the morning. Another day would have been intolerable.

"I don't think they'll be coming back soon," Blair murmured in the dark.

Nicky sighed. If only it were true. But it wasn't. Mildred would go home, regroup her forces, and be back next year. She was like the mailman, he thought. Neither rain nor snow nor sleet could keep her from her appointed rounds. He was on her route forever.

Blair was inching closer again. This time Nicky let him. He felt Blair's side touch his. A bit of familiar comfort oozed through him. "Feeling better?" Blair asked.

He wasn't but he said, "A little."

What was it about brothers and sisters? Was it natural to the relationship, or was there something especially ugly about him and Mildred? Shreds of Herbert's interminable story about his own sister came back to him. Herbert, believe it or not, had been jealous of her curls, which were modeled on Shirley Temple's. His mother had spent hours getting them in shape when company was coming.

He sighed again. Curls! If only it had been that simple!

Blair's hand was stealing over his chest, rubbing certain sensitive spots. He was grateful for the good intentions but he pushed Blair's hand gently away. He simply didn't have the energy for sex.

In the distance he heard a toilet flush. Mildred, probably. It had a relentlessly familiar sound and he realized that the characteristic house-noise of his childhood had been toilets flushing. His grandmother, his mother, his aunt, his sister—an infinite cycle of peeing and flushing. Now it had come to his own house, a continent away.

Blair's hand had snuck back and was gently roaming his chest. This time he let it remain. He felt the corners of his mind soften. He was beginning to relax.

And then, in a blaze of light, Bill Crooker appeared. Bill Crooker had been the boy he loved and Mildred—yes, Mildred!—had stolen him away. His legs stiffened, his back arched and he was instantly wide awake.

Bill Crooker! At the age of fourteen, his mind, his heart, his dreams, had all been bounded by Bill Crooker. He would do anything to get Bill's attention. He went to school hoping Bill would see him today, would sit with him in the cafeteria, would walk him home at three-thirty. Bill's broad shoulders, his manly gestures, his easy way with a joke, even the I.D. bracelet reposing carelessly on his left wrist—all these had a message especially for him. There was no joy to compare to being touched by Bill—even a push was better than nothing, but when Bill clapped his arm around his shoulder, or patted him on the back, he felt he had been singled out from every other boy in school in some sacred way.

He was suddenly aware that Blair's hand had moved to his groin and was doing some skillful manipulating down there. To his surprise, he was responding—in spite of his fatigue, his annoyance. Everything was a jumble in his mind, past and present, Mildred and Herbert, Blair and... yes, Bill Crooker.

Mildred had stolen him away. Yes, spitefully, triumphantly, stolen him as easily as the fairies kidnapped unwary children in his favorite stories. He had seen it happen, seen her coming home early when she knew Bill and he would be playing Monopoly, horned in on their game, teased Bill into giving her a ride in his jalopy, even made brownies for him! And the bitterest part was that he could tell no one, mention it to no other soul. He had never known such solitude, before or since.

Blair was leaning over and kissing him. His lips were soft. Nicky put his hand around the back of Blair's head and pressed as hard as he could.

One night he had crawled out of his bedroom window and leaned dangerously over the rain-gutter to watch Bill bring Mildred home from a dance—a dance which he had no wish to attend. He had wrapped himself around the rainspout and watched, his breath coming harshly, the sweat cold in the small of his back. He had watched Mildred being held in Bill's strong arms, receiving his kiss, listening to Bill's murmured endearments. And afterwards, back in bed, he had heard Mildred's light step on the stairs, had imagined Bill's imprint on her lips, Bill's musk on her thighs—and been choked with bitterness in the pennant-hung chamber of his adolescence.

They had their pajamas off, without his having noticed. "Oh God," he cried as he felt Blair's arms around him. "Oh God." And then they threw off the covers and went at it, the stars cold outside the bedroom window. Nicky buried his face in Blair's groin. What if he had made love to Bill? What if he and Bill had run away—hobos together, companions forever? What if Mildred had never scored her easy victory, *knowing exactly how he felt?*

And then he forgot all that in the panic of making love.

SHE'D BEEN RIGHT, of course. She couldn't sleep. Not a chance. Besides, the bed was saggy and there were bugs battering against the screen.

She rolled over, repressing a groan, aware of Herbert. He'd gone right to sleep. In a few minutes the snores would start.

She directed her thoughts carefully. She didn't want a lot of useless ideas cropping up in the dark. If she just let go, she wouldn't sleep a wink all night.

If only Nicky wouldn't bring up these childhood things! If only he would forget the past! What was the difference where Dranie was buried? Of couse, he was doing it to be unconventional. Nicky liked to do the unconventional thing, even though he was secretly respectable, secretly yearned to be accepted and approved.

She shifted position. She mustn't let her mind run away with her. Nicky was a good person. He even voted Republican half the time. She had wanted her boys to know their uncle. When they were younger, both Thaddeus and Pierce had come north to pay visits. And Nicky had put himself out—baseball games, auto races, even a trip to Yosemite. Of course, once the boys reached adolescence, she didn't encourage the visiting. You never know. Still, she was pleased they were all good friends now.

Maybe she should get up and heat herself a glass of milk. That might help. How stupid to forget her Dalmane. It was still sitting at home in the medicine chest, the little pills that spelled sleep...

There was that thing with Thaddeus. If she started thinking about that! Thaddeus was showing signs of being a weak reed too. There had been the trouble in the locker room at school. With a rush of pain she wondered if her genes were bad and if her boys had inherited them.

No, that was impossible. She didn't have an abnormal bone in her body. Nicky was a freak, an exception... besides, he simply indulged himself. If he'd put his mind to it, he could have married and produced children like everybody else.

The thought calmed her, and she felt a weariness pass through her. It had been a long day. But tomorrow she'd be home. Her eyelids were getting heavy. There was nothing to worry about. Thaddeus would get over it. It was just a phase. Very common. All the handbooks told you that.

She was right at the edge of sleep when she heard it. A faint thumping. At first she thought it was her heartbeat, but a moment later, her flesh went cold with dread. She knew exactly what it was and where it was coming from. She stared alertly into the darkness, sleep out of the question.

How could they? *How could they?*

She was having trouble breathing. Did they have no respect? No shame?

She sat up. "Herbert," she whispered. She poked him and he stirred.

And then, suddenly, she didn't want to wake him up. She didn't want him to hear those sounds. It was her side of the family causing the trouble. *Her* side! *Her* genes!

The thumping speeded up. She put her feet on the floor. There was only one thing to do. She stood, looking down at Herbert's dark form. For the first time in her married life she was too mortified to share her feelings with her husband.

She opened the door and glided out. Gathering her nightgown tightly around her breasts, she padded down the hall.

"Nicholas!" She rapped firmly on the door. "Nicholas!"

A voice came from inside. It was hoarse. She couldn't tell which one it belonged to. "What?"

"Will you please stop that?"

She heard whispers, curses. The door flung open. She stepped back. It was Nicky, totally nude, his body flashing with sweat. She covered her eyes.

"Stop what?" he hissed. He was furious. She stifled the impulse to run back and get Herbert.

"Stop what you're doing, please." She didn't take her hand away from her eyes.

"Why?"

She stepped back a few paces and looked. It was horrible. "How could you?" she said. "How could you while we're here?"

Nicky advanced toward her, lifting his arm. She had never seen him like this. She cowered against the wall. "It's my house, Mildred," he thundered, "and if you want me to drive you to a motel I will."

There was a frozen moment while she stared at him, then with a hollow cry, she turned and ran. In her room she fell into bed gasping and choking. A door slammed in the distance. Herbert woke up at last, but she couldn't tell him anything. Simply could... not. It was too shameful.

Because now she knew. Knew in spite of all her efforts to keep the knowledge at bay. Her family genes were rotten. Her boys were contaminated. And there was nothing she could do. She pressed her hand to her forehead and groaned. There was nothing she could do. Even her boys, her precious boys, carried inside them the seeds of their own destruction.

Nicky awoke with a jolt, instantly awake. Weak morning sun filtered through the curtains. Blair was on his side, hands between his legs, in a fetal crouch. For a moment Nicky couldn't remember why everything felt so unpleasant, then it came back in a rush.

Mildred! He flung his arm across his eyes, as if he could blot out the sight of her. Impossible. She was everywhere. Embarrassment and shame heated his face. How could he face her this morning?

Blair's breath rose and fell gently. Nicky watched, momentarily comforted. Thank heavens Blair was here. He hadn't stood by him in the restaurant—but he had lain by him and slept by him. That added up to the same thing. Maybe more. He rested his arm on Blair's shoulder, watching it move up and down with the breathing.

Of course, he and Blair had been unable to resume after the interruption. He'd wakened and masturbated into a Kleenex in the middle of the night, feeling furtive and nasty, just as he had in high school.

Well, Mildred had finally gotten the message. The cover-up had ended. Then, to his surprise, he felt slightly relieved. If only they could make a habit of scenes like that—scenes in which they stripped and shrieked and told the truth! He sighed. Impossible, of course.

He could hear the voices in the living room. Mildred and Herbert. They were probably packed and ready to go. Perched on the edge of the sofa, waiting for him to drive them to the airport. What on earth would he say?

And then, with a horrible certainty, he knew. They would say nothing. *Nothing.* It would all be wiped out, the tape rewound and erased. Last night would join the limbo of all the other family events which had to be ignored or forgotten. Conversation with Mildred would be impossible so Herbert would take over. Long, boring pointless stories which would permit Mildred and him to withdraw, to hide . . .

He slid out of bed, his heart pounding, and put on his bathrobe. He wasn't sure what he was going to do. Blair opened one eye. "Go back to sleep," Nicky whispered. Blair sighed and turned over.

They were sitting on the couch in the living room. Mildred was very pale, dark smudges under her eyes. Herbert's blue eyes seemed buried in layers of cheek.

"Good morning." It was Mildred, her voice full of injury.

"Good morning." His heart was pounding quite hard now.

"We called a taxi, no use bothering you." Herbert waved his hand and smiled.

"I can drive you."

"Nah."

Nicky looked at his sister. "How do you feel?"

"Not very well." Her tone, he realized, was meant to induce guilt by its quiet bravery. But strangely, he didn't feel guilty. Instead, he felt an insane urge to laugh. His heart had stopped pounding and the room in which they sat seemed suddenly flooded with beauty. Looking at their figures, poised on the edge of the couch, he realized that he loved this room, this house, and that neither Mildred nor Herbert would ever really belong in it.

"There's something I want to tell you, Mill." His voice was light and dry.

She looked at him sharply. "You don't have to apologize."

He laughed at that, quite loudly, and her eyes widened. "I wasn't going to," he said. "I was going to tell you something else."

He watched Mildred shift position nervously. Perhaps he had already transmitted part of his message. "Did you know I was in love with Bill Crooker?" His voice was still light and pleasant. Mildred's eyes widened some more. "I loved him for years and years. I still love him."

The words, he knew, sounded absurdly irrelevant in the morning light of California, but he didn't care. He went on. "I never told anyone. Not a soul. I couldn't. Not even when you took him away."

She made a sudden movement, putting her hand to her cheek and Nicky knew she had understood.

"It's not important now," he concluded. "I just thought I'd like to tell you. We've both kept it a secret so long." He paused, aware of joy flowering all around him. "You and me, Mill. All these years."

The room was silent. He stood up, wondering if there was anything more to say. "Oh yes," he added, "I don't think I want to drive you to the airport after all." He smiled and started out. Glancing back, he saw they were sitting still as statues.

In the bathroom, he emptied his bladder, enjoying the noise of his stream of urine. Then he washed his face and combed his hair, searching the mirror for some difference that would match the change within. Nothing. The same face, hair, eyes. The same expression—smooth, benign. Surely his face should read differently now. But no, there was no outward change. Maybe he was really the same. Maybe he was now, at last, himself.

He smiled at the thought, then laughed outright. He had just imagined his death and his burial in the cemetery next to his grandparents, now joined in death as they had been in life thanks to something so simple as a forged signature on a release. And, in perfect detail, the legend on his tombstone came to him: Here Lies the Baddest Penny, the Baddest Faggot, the Baddest Jew.

He waited in the bathroom, studying his reflection, until he heard footsteps in the hallway, then the closing of the front door. When the house was still, he went to start coffee for Blair and himself.

As the plane took off, Mildred closed her eyes and reached for Herbert's hand. It held hers reassuringly. When the worst of the thunder was over she opened her eyes. A steward was bending over them. He reminded her of Nicky or one of his friends, she couldn't say exactly why.

"Coffee for you folks?"

So he had remembered Bill Crooker! So long ago, a lifetime ago! He'd carried it around with him all these years, waiting to bring it up. She could hardly remember Bill now, except that he wore a blue-and-white striped polo shirt and had an I.D. bracelet of silver. How childish it had all been.

She looked at Herbert, who was eyeing one of the boxes of little liquor bottles. She'd have to prevent that.

Bill Crooker! Is that what Nicky had been sulling about all these years? Of course she knew about their romance, so-called. She'd come home one afternoon and found them side by side on the sofa with the shades pulled down. The room simply reeked of mischief. She'd told mother about it right away, but mother had gotten her mysterious look and told her not to worry about it.

What Nicky didn't know was that Bill was afraid of him. Afraid of Nicky's moony stares and sneaky rubs and suggestions that they run away together. She had actually saved Bill from Nicky.

The steward returned with the coffee. From the way he smiled and wiggled she knew why he looked familiar. He was one of *them*. Of course.

Nicky thought you could settle accounts with the past, tidy up the loose ends. But you couldn't, not by digging up Dranie, Bill Crooker or anybody else. When would he learn that?

Never. He would never learn. He would make and remake the world, folding it over and over in his mind until he got a pattern he liked. But it would never be the right pattern. The true pattern.

The true pattern came from being part of the great cycle of family life. Suddenly she saw mother and Dranie and all the other women in her family holding hands and reaching back, back as far as she could see. She held up her hand as if to link herself to them, but dropped it, feeling a little silly. Then she leaned over and told Herbert he couldn't have a drink until they got home.

She was beginning to feel a little better at last. She thought she would probably never come back to San Francisco.

A Touch of Fat

It would soon be all right, Frady reminded himself as he strained to see over the crowd at Gate 18. Around him, hordes of Puerto Ricans, brilliant in multicolored clothes, were chattering excitedly. He had never known people who talked so much. They nattered, they sang, they chirped. They did everything but stand still and listen. But that wasn't quite fair. Sometimes, when least expected, they did stand still, with the stillness of a lizard on a jungle leaf. This was equally disconcerting.

The loudspeaker boomed in Spanish and Frady's heart gave a little tug. The prospect of seeing Tom, of course. Seeing that familiar craggy face with the jutting chin, here in San Juan. It would be strange at first. But within minutes the strangeness would disappear and a fine familiarity would take its place. They would be instantly at home. Sometimes Frady thought that he and Tom carried home around with them, like two snails each with half a shell. Home was the place where they came together.

His recent troubles, he reflected, would evaporate. Wasn't that why he had urged Tom to spend Christmas here? Because Tom carried the remedies in his brown eyes, his quiet hands, his even voice?

The first passengers from Flight 63 filed past, pale from the northern cold. Frady's sense of homecoming increased. Tom was only a few steps away now. His sensory antennae had always been tuned to Tom. Once, at the very moment Tom was writing a letter to him from New Hampshire (he later found out) his own mind went into a spasm of receptivity and the window shade in his apartment in New York rolled up with a fierce splat. It was their private radio band sparking. When he had told Tom about this, Tom had smiled condescendingly—Frady and his psychokinesis!—but Frady hadn't been put off. He knew they got signals from each other on secret frequencies. He knew now, for example, that Tom would appear before he could count to ten. He closed his eyes.

"Hello Frady." He opened his eyes. Tom was at his side, smiling weakly and looking nonchalant. Important moments made Tom nonchalant unless he broke down and cried. Frady read his face as if it were a map to buried treasure. Then he reached out and hugged him tightly.

How well he knew that body! He imagined it again, not as he could feel it now—slightly saggy in the tits, the belly a little basketball, the hips lightly sheathed in fat—but as it had been twenty years ago when he had first glimpsed it. That had been in Tom's little apartment near Gramercy Park in New York. When they had stripped in the bedroom under a bare light bulb dangling from a long cord, he had scarcely been able to draw breath at the sight of Tom nude, at the wide bony shoulders, the triangle of black chest-hair, the square pectorals, the powerfully fleshed calves. But it was something else that had taken his breath away, that had convinced him that Tom (whose last name he had yet to learn) was the most beautiful man he had ever encountered. This something else was the gaunt boniness of Tom's face, the hollowness of his cheeks, the secret caverns of his collarbones, the shadowy recesses of his pelvis. Tom, he had realized with a pang, was a scarecrow of bone and sinew. He might have been a half-starved Okie in the depths of the depression, caught for a tragic moment in the glare of Margaret Bourke-White's camera.

Later, after he and Tom had begun to live together, he had wondered at his taste for scarecrows, for Lincolnesque men, long-muscled and rifle-thin, and why that gaunt look signaled to him so deeply. But he had never been able to sort it out, never been able to trace it to some early impression or to some childish love. These men attracted him—he had known it when he was ten or twelve—but it wasn't until he met Tom Peniman in a bar on Eighth Street that he had realized the extent of his addiction. Sometimes, lying in bed with Tom in that first home they had shared, it seemed that all his life had been tending toward this time, and that whoever he was, wherever he had come from, could be summed up in his passion for the gaunt male lying next to him.

They were headed for the luggage area of the airport now, walking easily in step. Tom was talking about the flight from Los Angeles. Frady noticed that he had put on some more weight in the last year. His eyes seemed to have receded even more behind the bulge of his cheeks. His walk was more turned out than before. Without looking, Frady could sense the extra fat around his hips and ass. But even as he registered this, he dismissed the knowledge as disloyal. Tom hadn't changed, not really. Under the extra flesh were the bones, the osteal fragments that spelled love. It was just a matter of getting through to them.

Tom was discussing the in-flight movie. He had seen it before, to his disappointment. As Frady listened, he recalled how Tom always talked—never shouting for attention, never raising his voice. He felt something inside him thaw out, something that had been frozen for a long time.

Frady chose the scenic route for the drive to the apartment. In the car, they caught up on people, places, events. Although they wrote each other every week, letters couldn't take the place of being together, hearing each other's voice. At one point, as they passed a crescent of beach, a wave soared up and broke into pieces a few yards away. "Look at that," Tom said in his flat voice, and it seemed to Frady that the surf had never been so beautiful, that he had never enjoyed it so much.

Tom settled into the second bedroom right away. The

room became instantly messy. Messy and lived-in, Frady thought. It should have been that way right along. But he had kept it bare, impersonal. There had been a few guests from the States, a few island friends, but their traces had been quickly removed. Even the party he gave for his students at the end of the term, which had overflowed into this bedroom, hadn't disorganized it as Tom did. No one could appropriate space in his life in quite the same way. It had been like that from the very beginning.

A week after they had met, twenty years ago, Tom had moved in with him, giving up the little apartment on Gramercy Park and arriving at Frady's West Side apartment with the instinct of a homing pigeon. Frady had never shared so much of his life before. At first it was hard. Unlike Tom, who came from a large Iowa family, his own had been small and divided. His one brother, older than he, had been his bitter enemy for as long as he could remember. On the savage stomping grounds of childhood they had competed for everything—for love, attention, grades, friends, home runs. Their childhoods had been scarred by a bitter mutual contempt. The causes were obscure, but the result was not. He had avoided an intimate relationship with anyone his own age until he was thirty, until he met Tom Peniman in a Village bar and went home with him, overcoming his fear of intimacy, of rejection, of *family,* only slowly, over the months.

Tom, he had realized at once, wanted to become his family, wanted to extend their natural fit in bed to the rest of their lives. To sharing the medicine chest and doing laundry together. To drinking and quarreling and wearing each other's clothes. To traveling and cooking and writing sonnets in alternate lines. This was all new to Frady. He had always protected his privacy, ever since the morning when he was five years old and had refused to share a bathtub with his brother, furious at the thought of sitting in *his* water, kicking and screaming until his mother had given in. Since then, the privacy had thickened around him like a fog, inside of which he moved, with all his deepest feelings veiled from view. Tom had punched a hole in that fog—he himself had been more than ready, of course—until it had evaporated altogether. Tom's simple assumption that Frady could share his life had made it possible to do so.

Tom was a poet. He had shown Frady a huge sheaf of poems on their first morning after. They seemed wonderfully fresh and new, with a kind of sweet innocence he would always associate with Tom. Tom, he realized after reading the poems, was not shored up with defenses like most people. He was without affectation or guile. "He has a good heart," he had once said to a friend. Of course, that was too simple. Over the months and years he would find Tom far more complex, with a dark side as well as a bright one. But under the shadows he always saw the sweetness. He believed in Tom's good heart the way he believed in his mother's love and in democracy. It made sense of the world.

They decided to have a swim before lunch. Tom squinted against the glare when they stepped outside. They had a race to the water, but Frady won easily. He was still slender and fast on his feet, his body (thanks to years of gym-work) sleek and full of tone. Tom, he could see, waddled as much as he ran, the extra flesh rippling around his stomach and hips. He tripped when he hit the water and pitched forward.

"Oh wow, I hit something," he said, coming up and blowing water.

"You went in like an old sea cow," Frady yelled.

"Fuck you," Tom called back. Frady plunged into an oncoming wave. When he surfaced, Tom was heading toward the reef. Frady noted that he still swam well, his weight buoyed up by the water, his strokes slow and graceful.

Treading water, Frady glanced toward shore. A Chinese wall of condominiums ringed the beach. In front, spotting the sand, were hundreds of brown bodies. He knew those bodies. Many of them were exquisitely made. The sight forced into his mind something he had been dodging all day.

He reached for it now, reassured by the nearness of Tom. Suppose he and Tom were to get together again! The thought caused a moment's panic, and he spun around in the water. Then the anxiety cleared and a vision sparkled brightly on the waves. Tonight. As they were getting ready for bed. A simple need. A simple act. They were better friends now than before—friends in a way they could not be when they lived together. Passion and jealousy had obscured the fineness of their feeling for each other, the fit of their minds, their spirits. Why not convert that friendship back into something physical?

He thought about the power of Tom's presence. He was always strengthened by it, purified. Tom's sweetness called out his own. He was, quite simply, a better person when Tom was around. His pettiness, his spite—all the unpleasant sides of his personality—dissipated in Tom's bright sunshine. Couldn't that be part of his life again, permanently? He thought about the bleakness of things since he had turned fifty a few months ago. Wouldn't that be wiped out too?

He floated on his back and stared at the sky. What was it the physicists said when their theories were especially apt? He searched for the word. *Elegant.* That was it. Reconverting their friendship into passion would be... *elegant.*

He turned over and let a monster wave carry him to shore.

FRADY WATCHED TOM carefully over dinner. He had fixed a Puerto Rican meal, taken from *Cocina Criolla*. On the plates were arroz con pollo, fried bananas and chayote. Tom, who had slept all afternoon, was looking refreshed. Some of the lines cut into his cheeks and chin had begun to soften. In a few days, Frady knew, he would look much younger. Tom wore a flowered Hawaiian shirt which glowed in the candlelight.

"Remember that first Thanksgiving on 88th Street?" Frady asked.

Tom nodded.

"It was the most beautiful meal I'd ever had."

"It was okay."

"Okay!" Frady was outraged. The old memories hadn't excited Tom tonight. He had spent most of the meal reminiscing, but Tom had added little. He decided to give it another try.

"After we set the table you said, 'Let's just stand here and admire it, it looks like a Norman Rockwell painting.' "

Tom grimaced. "I always hated Norman Rockwell." he pushed the food around on his plate. He hadn't eaten much. Too starchy probably, Frady thought. "What are we going to do tonight?" Tom asked.

"I thought we'd stay home and take it easy."

Tom took a sip of wine. "We've been home all day." He knitted his brows. "Why don't we go to the casino?" He looked up, his brown eyes alight. "Hey, I haven't been to a casino in a long time."

Frady thought distastefully of the hotels, which would be filled with tourists in cruisewear. But Tom was on his feet, peering out the window. "Which is better, El San Juan or the Hilton?"

"They're all the same," Frady said petulantly, but Tom didn't seem to notice his tone.

"Dress up, baby," he crowed in a voice Frady had never heard before. "I'm gonna make us some house money!"

He turned around. Frady blinked rapidly. Tom's face seemed to have taken on a new shape. It had broadened, fattened. It was almost as round and fat as a basketball. Frady blinked some more, trying to chase the image away. Maybe it was a trick of the candlelight. He looked away, then back. There. That was better. The roundness seemed not to have disappeared exactly, but... condensed. Yes, there was the face he knew so well. Gaunt, cavernous. He stared hard, fixing it, in case the basketball look came back again.

Tom started to clear the table. "That was good, Frady, but I just wasn't hungry, I guess."

Frady knew the signs. Tom would fix himself a large salad in an hour and top it off with some dried prunes and a box of fig newtons. Luckily, he had laid in the necessary supplies. He sighed and got up. The casino seemed unavoidable.

T OM WAS IN HIGH SPIRITS as they walked toward the hotel, bouncing along the pavement, pointing to the palms, the prostitutes, the cars packed with Puerto Rican teenagers. Suddenly he started to sing. *"Asturias, patria querida... Asturias, de mis amores..."* The melody surged through Frady. It was a song they had learned in Mallorca, in the tiny mountain village where they had lived for six months. Someone had taught it to them in the village café, where they had been drinking Fundador after a day spent visiting the monastery where Chopin had lived with George Sand.

"God," he said, "I haven't heard that in years."

"Haven't sung it in years," Tom replied. He went into the second verse—he had an amazing memory for lyrics—and some Puerto Ricans in a passing car let out a whoop. *"Hola!"* Tom cheered, waving back.

Frady felt drenched with nostalgia. Mallorca! Could it have been eighteen years ago? They had taken up residence in a handsome house with blue shutters, surrounded by the sound of sheep bells and the silvery flutter of olive groves. They had made love almost constantly in the upstairs bedroom.

"Here we are!" Tom's yelp interrupted his reverie. The hotel lobby loomed in front of them. Its furniture seemed designed for a race of giants. Tom speeded up. "Next time you come out to California I'll take you to Las Vegas," he called back over his shoulder.

Frady snickered. Las Vegas wasn't high on his list of desirable experiences. "I'd rather go back to Ensenada," he replied. They passed two bouncers at the door to the casino.

"There's nothing to do in Ensenada," Tom announced just before disappearing into the crowd.

Frady watched him go, thinking about the little village where they had lived in Mallorca. There hadn't been much to do there either. No movies, no concerts, no casinos. They didn't even have a radio. What had they done all day? He searched his memory. They had looked at the vines and flowers. Tom had worked on his poems. He had learned Spanish guitar. They had taken long hikes over the stony soil. They had invited their neighbors for tea. They had made love. Was that all?

He saw Tom in the distance, at a blackjack table. He seemed to have bought some chips already. The unpleasant notion inserted itself into Frady's mind that Tom had changed. That he wasn't the exact person he had always been. The old Tom had hated plastic environments like this. He'd pass up a casino for a poetry reading any day. And there he was, chatting with a burly croupier and watching the drop of the cards as if he were Nick the Greek. It was very puzzling.

Frady drifted over to the slot machines. He liked to watch the players. They were mostly elderly women holding plastic glasses full of quarters, which they fed into the machines with a drugged air. He wondered if his own life would end up that way—an idle search for the excitement that sex and friendship and a career could no longer provide. He shuddered at the thought. And then, without warning, the bleakness of the past few months hit him again. Instinctively, as despair spread through him, he sifted through the crowd, looking for Tom. Where was he?

Frady moved to get a better view across the room. *Where was he?* There he was, at the roulette table, standing behind a woman with red hair. Frady watched him accept two black chips from her and lay them on the cloth. The woman laughed and offered Tom a cigarette. Frady watched numbly as Tom took it. The two put their heads together for a light.

And then, by a strange alteration, it seemed to Frady that Tom had grown shorter and fatter. At the same time, his hairline moved upward, although it was possible his face had slipped downward instead. Then it struck him that the short fat man across the room was someone he had never seen before. The confusion made him slightly dizzy. He felt as if a crack had opened in the world, a huge crack that might never be closed if he didn't move carefully in the next few seconds. He moved rapidly across the room.

"Tom." Tom, his eyes on the roulette wheel, didn't turn around. Frady pinched his arm. "I'm leaving," he said. The ball had settled into a groove but the wheel was spinning too fast to read the number. "I'm going home," Frady said.

Suddenly Tom let out a cry. "We won!" He threw his arms around the woman with red hair, who shrieked. Tom turned around. His eyes were glazed. "We won!" he cried again, but he seemed to be addressing everybody, not just Frady.

Frady left the casino without actually deciding to do so. His feet simply carried him out the door. His last sight of Tom was as he placed another bet on the green cloth. He looked, Frady thought, like a shoe salesman who had just sold an especially expensive pair of shoes.

Frady drifted along the pavement, vaguely aware of the sound of the surf on his left, of a tree frog striking its tiny marimba across the street. A huge emptiness seemed to have blown into his chest. Several times he had to stop walking to fight the sensation of falling through it. If he didn't have Tom, what did he have? Could he survive?

When he reached his corner and turned toward the apartment, he shook his head briskly. He had to get control of himself. It was absurd to be so dependent on Tom. That suffocating dependence had been the reason for their break-up in the first place. They had almost smothered each other to death. What was it he had written in his diary during that last unhappy year? "Together we make one person, and that's the problem." Wasn't he doing the same thing now? Being childish and jealous and possessive? Of course Tom had changed. You change in order to survive. Tom was no longer the young poet. How much poetry is left at fifty?

By the time he reached the door to his apartment he felt a little better. It was a case of facing facts. His wrinkles were facts. His slow sexual reflexes were facts. Time and change and the end of illusion were facts.

But even as he reminded himself of these things, an image

formed in his mind—or rather, a series of images complete to the tiniest detail. It had been on the ship that took them from New York to Mallorca. One night he had gone to bed early, tired of the endless cardgames and boozing. It seemed he had slept only a few hours when he heard Tom's voice breaking into his sleep. "Frady, Frady, wake up!" The voice was flushed, excited. "You have to come on deck!" Tom had kept shaking him until Frady got up and went with him through the deserted passage to the deck. He had followed Tom's slender, muscular figure to the bow and there Tom had pointed to a dim shape on the starboard side. It was a landmass, faintly illuminated by dawn. "Look," Tom's breath was warm in his ear, "Africa!"

And he had looked at the dark shape as images and associations thundered in his head. "I stayed up all night," Tom murmured, "I was afraid I'd miss it."

And then, quite without thinking, they had reached out and taken hands, heedless of who might be watching, as the ship throbbed under them and Africa took shape in the dawn. Tom's hand had been warm and papery, but Frady had sensed the wild pulse beating, had understood Tom's feelings because they were as important as his own. And he had known that this moment would always stay with them, that some part of them would always be on the deck of this ship, holding hands while Africa grew large in the dawn and the morning star winked out.

Later, they had gone to sleep in the single lower bunk of their cabin, entwined together, neither wanting to spend the rest of the night alone.

Now, standing in the middle of his living room, Frady asked himself if the man who had stayed awake all night for a first glimpse of Africa could ever be a stranger. Could ever change, deeply and truly. He knew the answers to that as surely as he knew anything in the world.

T OM DIDN'T COME BACK until almost two. Frady had dozed off on the couch after fixing himself a rum and tonic. When he heard the downstairs bell, he woke up and moved to the buzzer. Tom stepped from the elevator with a fuzzy air. He and the red-headed woman had won almost a thousand dollars. They had been drinking Rémy-Martin in the hotel bar.

Frady waited while Tom went to the bathroom, then into the bedroom. When he heard the bed squeak as Tom sat down, he went in. Without speaking, he began to unbutton his shirt.

"What're you doing?" Tom's speech was slurred.

Frady found himself suddenly nervous. "I thought... I thought I'd rest with you a bit." He paused, then more softly, "Like old times."

He felt, rather than saw, Tom studying him.

"Just for a few minutes," he whispered, feeling like a liar.

Tom stood up and disrobed slowly. Frady moved onto the bed, stretching out against the wall. He had always slept on the inside of any bed with Tom. It made him feel safe.

Tom was down to his boxer shorts. Frady could see that the skin on his stomach was shiny and tight over the bulge. Briefly he thought of a pregnant woman.

Tom's weight on the bed made Frady tilt toward him. He started to roll downhill, then grabbed the far edge of the mattress and hoisted himself back. Tom settled himself on his back. Frady waited a moment, then dropped one arm lightly across Tom's chest. "This feels so good," he breathed. Tom grunted and put his arm over his eyes.

"I was thinking..." Frady paused. Tom grunted again. "I was thinking we haven't given ourselves a chance in years." His hand, automatically, had started rubbing Tom's chest, pulling at the triangular patch of hair which, he had noticed earlier in the day, was now quite gray. He moved to Tom's left nipple. It was the size of a raisin and had always been amazingly sensitive. Tom twitched briefly. Frady watched Tom's other arm—not the one over his eyes—move down to the groin and start a regular rhythm.

His heart beating rapidly, Frady slipped out of his underwear. Tom turned toward him. Their mouths searched and found each other. As they kissed, Frady felt an easing through his whole body. It seemed that he had traveled for years and only now come home. Tom's arms encircled him. The sense of homecoming increased.

Tom started to vibrate his body against Frady's. *Jiggle jiggle jiggle* went Tom's body. Frady could hear the slap of Tom's stomach as it hit his own. He pushed lightly against Tom's heavy form. This was not exactly what he had in mind. Tom's stomach heaved and quivered some more. *Jiggle jiggle jiggle.* Frady pushed away a little harder. The slapping sound grew louder. It seemed to have nothing to do with sex. Frady had the feeling he was being buried in a hill of flesh. At the same time he was aware that the tingling in his own groin had stopped. Nothing was happening down there. "Oh Christ," he said out loud.

The jiggling stopped. "What's the matter?"

"I don't know."

"Well let's go."

"I don't like that."

"Like what?"

"Rubbing bellies."

There was a silence and he could hear Tom's raspy breathing. "You started this whole thing," he mumbled.

"I'm sorry. I . . . just . . ."

A sound came out of Tom, halfway between a snort and a bellow, and he tightened his grip around Frady's middle. At the same time he hoisted himself up. Frady felt Tom's body slide over his. He suddenly had the feeling he was at the bottom of a vegetable bin. *Jiggle jiggle jiggle.* It had started again. Frady had a wild urge to shove Tom off and leap out of bed. But then, by a powerful effort of will, he mastered the urge. Instead, he decided to think about something else. Mallorca. Of course, Mallorca! The upstairs bedroom where they had kissed and grappled and hugged the night away. He kept his mind trained on this, not hearing the slapping noises, not feeling the thumps of Tom's body, as he remembered

Tom's long lean muscles, the bones that clicked under the skin, the orgasms that slid out of them in tongues of fire...

The jiggling wasn't getting any faster. What was going on? In the old days it never took Tom long to come. And his back was beginning to hurt. He'd end up at the orthopedist again if he wasn't careful. Still, he didn't want to be selfish...

He twisted his mind back to the bedroom in Mallorca. But it seemed to have slid away. Disappeared completely. He was here, now, with the dead sound of Tom's thumping in his ears.

He waited. Time seemed to have stopped. The thumping went on. Tom's breathing got heavier, raspier. He waited some more.

"Tom," he whispered. There was no answer. "Can you come?"

There was still no answer and suddenly he couldn't bear another second of it. He pushed Tom hard. The heavy body fell to one side.

"I can't do it any more," he growled.

"Whaddya mean?" Tom's voice was faint, almost sleepy.

"I just can't. Can not." He sat up. Across the hall his own bedroom glowed in the dark.

"I was almost there," Tom moaned.

Frady scrambled out of bed. "No you weren't. You were miles away." He was surprised at the coldness of his voice.

Tom twisted onto his back. He seemed totally inert, like a sack of grain. Frady, looking down at him, wondered how he had ever thought they could get together. And then their failure in bed seemed to grow in size and darkness until it cast a pall over everything between them. He felt himself moving away from the figure on the bed. There was no link, no bridge. Tom had changed, he had changed. He was living in the past, but there was nothing there. The old fantasies were finished. He was alone. He would have to face everything alone...

Suddenly he realized that Tom was crying. He turned. Tom's face was bright with tears. "Don't cry," he said. But the tears kept flowing. "Tom," he pleaded. "Tom."

Tom lay there, not speaking. The tears ran down his face and dripped on the sheet. He made no effort to wipe them away. And then Frady, with a wrench, realized that Tom was crying for both of them. His tears bathed them both. The realization came to him in a rush of joy. Tom might have given up poetry and taken up gambling, he might be fat and fifty, he might be finished with nostalgia and illusion... but his heart was the same. It was still good. And if that was so, there was nothing to be afraid of. The world still made sense.

His last sight was of Tom lying in bed, weeping and jerking off.

They didn't talk much in the morning. Frady felt raw, as if a wound had opened in the night. At the same time, everything seemed very vivid—the furniture, the food, the sea and sky. He knew it was the same for Tom.

About noon they decided to go for a swim. On the way, they talked of unimportant things, but Frady found himself getting worked up even about these. As they headed across the sand for the water, Tom said nonchalantly, "I knew you had that in mind as soon as I got off the plane."

Frady froze. "You what?"

Tom chuckled. "Fucking. I knew you had it in mind."

"How did you know? I didn't even know myself."

"Just did." Tom frowned. "I had the feeling it wouldn't work."

"You sneaky bastard, why didn't you say something?"

Tom shrugged. "I figured we would just see what happened." His voice was mild. "Just... let go." He searched Frady's face and Frady knew he could read everything there. A delicious calm took possession of him. They still understood each other perfectly. There was nothing they might not say or do together. They might even—he giggled slightly—repeat last night's fiasco. It would still be okay. It would always be okay.

"Bet I can beat you in," Tom said suddenly. He lurched toward the water. "The hell you can," Frady roared. And then he gave chase—the sand hot under his feet, the air bright around him, the fat familiar body just ahead rippling with love.

The Boy
Who Would Be Real

WARREN READ THE STORY of Pinocchio when he was ten years old. There were words he didn't understand, but he got the main point right away: Pinocchio was not a real boy. He was carved out of wood. He couldn't run or ride a bike. He couldn't kiss his mother or spread strawberry jam on bread. The thought that Pinocchio might remain a piece of wood forever filled Warren with pain. It seemed the most terrifying thing that could happen.

Many years later, when he was middle-aged and living in California, he recalled the anguish he felt as he sat in the low velvet chair in the sun-parlor, the blue volume on his lap, the light streaking the floor. Suppose Pinocchio didn't become a real boy! Suppose he remained a block of wood! Looking back, he saw that his own predicament at the age of ten had somehow gotten mixed up with Pinocchio's. They were both in mortal danger.

The year before, when he was nine, he had been sitting quietly in his room drawing pictures of girls in beautiful flowing gowns when his father appeared. His father was a thick man who wore red suspenders and had hairs growing from the tip of his nose. Now he peered through his silver-rimmed spectacles at Warren's drawing and said, "For Christ's sake, why can't you be a real boy? Why can't you be like Ronnie?"

His father popped his eyes, scowled and walked out. A few

minutes later, Warren heard the baseball game coming from his father's radio. He sat for a long time, the beautiful reds and purples on the page in front of him suddenly sad and smeary, then got up and went to the mirror. It was a critical moment in his childhood. For the first time, he saw that he was not a real boy, and that this was reflected in what he saw. Although he could see his dark hair and brown eyes and round face, they no longer enclosed anything definite. What he saw was just a bunch of air shaped into a face, the way a gingerbread man was a bunch of dough shaped into a face. There was no one inside.

He knew that if his cousin Ronnie, whom his father admired so much, were standing next to him, Ronnie's face would look very firm and precise. Ronnie, who was sturdy and athletic, would never be a nebulous blob.

He did not share with anyone the discovery that he was not a real boy. His mother, he knew, would have pooh-poohed it. But he checked the mirror every morning and evening, hoping that things would change. The night before his tenth birthday, he decided that the next morning—when his age had two numbers instead of one—he would become a real boy. This had happened, it seemed, to several of his classmates. The first thing he did on his birthday morning, even before opening the presents stacked under his bed, was to check the mirror. But he saw only the same face—large-eyed, pudgy, unappealing. Nothing had changed.

He was relieved to discover, on finishing *Pinocchio,* that the block of wood had become a real boy after all. Pinocchio had managed this as a reward for saving Geppetto from a shark. The book informed him that children who loved their parents, especially if they were sick or poor, always ended well. That night Warren lay in bed for a long time thinking of ways he could help his parents. Although they weren't sick or poor—far from it—there were certain things he could do. For example, his mother was always saying, "Pick that up," when she saw a bit of lint on the rug. Usually he pretended not to hear but now, he decided, he would obey her instantly.

He also resolved to mow the lawn without being asked.

As for his father, there was no question about what would please him—taking a boxing class at the YMCA. There had been angry discussions about this but Warren had always managed to get out of boxing lessons. He could do this because his mother backed him up. She approved his decision to take Beads and Leatherwork at the Y instead. His father would pop his eyes and scowl and there the matter would end. Now, he saw, the time had come to sign up for boxing.

The class was held in the basement of the YMCA every Saturday morning—a sinister place full of ropes and weights and pulleys, reminding Warren of a medieval torture chamber. He had known in advance that he could never learn how to box, and this was confirmed immediately. He usually stood in the ring, his arms waving as if he were batting flies, while fists flew at him from every direction and the coach yelled, "Cover your face, dammit." Warren accepted the beatings philosophically, knowing they would bring him one step closer to his goal.

This period of his life peaked when his father came to an exhibit bout and sat on a stool just outside the ring and watched Warren get smashed by Joe Torcello, a small hairy boy he particularly feared. After his nose began to bleed, the coach stopped the fight and everyone cheered. Then the coach told his father he was a tough little scrapper. His father was so pleased that he said, "Wipe that blood off your face and I'll buy you a present." Then he took Warren to a shoe store and bought him a new pair of sneakers. As they drove home, his father became friendlier than Warren could ever remember, and told him bloodthirsty stories about Jack Dempsey. Warren arrived home in a state of great elation and went directly to the mirror in his bedroom. He found, as he expected, that his face, which still had a few crusts of blood under the nose, had taken on a modest new firmness. After studying it for a while, though, he decided that the important thing had not changed. He was still not a real boy.

He wondered what to do next. He couldn't take much

more smashing up in boxing class. And he couldn't go back to Beads and Leatherwork, which was filled with undesirable types he had now outdistanced. That left football and baseball. His father was crazy about football and baseball.

Warren played a lot of team sports through junior high school. He always turned up for practice on time, toting the bats and extra shoulder pads, keeping track of the scores when everyone else forgot. But he was an unreliable player. He would drop easy flies, strike out, or miss a ball carrier coming right at him. On the other hand, he sometimes had good days, when his running brought forth cheers or when he hit home runs. After a good day, he would go home for a session with the mirror, and would notice some improvement. However, any change for the better would disappear after one of his bad days—simply melt away leaving him exactly the same. After several years of this he decided he wasn't getting anywhere. The bad days just canceled out the good days. It was time to give up team sports. His father, he knew, wouldn't really care, having decided his son would never be a first-class athlete.

In high school, Warren went out for cross-country, because it allowed him to be alone in the woods. He usually got a stitch about halfway through the course. "You gotta run through a stitch," the coach would tell them later, in the locker room, but Warren never could. The pain in his side was like an unscalable wall; it simply stopped him in his tracks. Needless to say, his failure at cross-country didn't help him with the mirror.

Soon after giving up running, Warren noticed that the boys who seemed most powerful and assured, who swaggered through the school halls in beefy majesty, spoke of their ability to drink. It struck Warren that if he couldn't be an athlete, he could get drunk. This required no special aptitude.

Accordingly, he arranged to turn up in the roadhouses where his classmates did their weekend drinking. He found it easy to drink as much as they did and, after eight or ten pitchers of beer had been consumed by all, he would become loud and obscene. He was thrilled by the easy camaraderie of the table, and he realized that the secret of being a real boy was to have real boys for friends. Looking around at his new boon companions, he knew that his father would be pleased. He was definitely moving toward his goal.

When he got home on Saturday night—usually throwing up along the way—he would stare at himself in the glass with something like arrogance. His face had lost its pudginess and had slimmed into a not unattractive boniness. However, if he stared long enough, he always found something around the eyes that was unsatisfactory—a cloudiness, a lurking fearfulness, a void. When he met this quality, which lived very far back in the mirror, his arrogance would fade and he would tumble into bed with the old feeling of failure. He still hadn't licked the problem. He was still not a real boy.

Warren went away to college when he was sixteen. One of the Ivy League schools accepted him. As he sat on the train for Boston, after having said goodbye to his father in Grand Central, he sensed that now, at last, he was on the verge of success. He was due to become a college man. This was a very definite condition, one that left no room for vagueness or unreality. A new identity hovered over him as the train clicked over the rails. It was just a matter of thinking and feeling like a college man. He began to practice speaking with a broad *a,* which seemed like a sensible first step. By the time he got to South Station, he was sure he'd made progress.

Warren knew right away that the two roommates assigned him by the college would not help him succeed in his quest. Their names were Dudley and Morgan and they were definitely Beads and Leatherwork types. Warren decided to go after the prep school graduates who seemed to have arrived in large, gabbling coveys and signed up for strange games like rugby and lacrosse. Making friends with them took time, of course, since Warren had to learn new modes of social communication, stripping away the morose and solitary habits of his boyhood and training himself in the use of wit, irony and ennui. But in time he managed all this and found himself moving in circles that were unquestionably desirable.

One of the high points of his early years in college was a cocktail party given after a football game with his school's archrival. As he saw his rooms crowd up with classmates and dates who were flush with excitement and elegance, he was filled with a cool pride. It was a victory to have lured them here, a sign that he was now, truly, a college man. These new friends talked of sailing cup races and Wimbledon, of sojourns at the Georges Cinq and skiing in the Dolomites. How far he had come since his Beads and Leatherwork days, or since his roadhouse drinking days! As he watched them consume the fishhouse punch he had mixed, and honk at each other, he felt like a character in an F. Scott Fitzgerald novel. For a while the sense of his own reality was overpowering. At last he had found a place where he belonged.

But as the party wore on and the girls' lipstick got smeared and their sweaters disarranged, as the boys grew louder and more grabby, Warren began to wonder if he were as closely linked to these people as he'd thought. He certainly didn't feel like pawing the girls. And they all seemed totally oblivious of him—as if, he thought, they were in a bar or restaurant rather than in his home. As these doubts grew, he felt his connection with his guests grow more tenuous. Their reality was stronger than his despite all his efforts. This discovery depressed him so much that he stopped ladling the punch and went into the bedroom and sat among the scarves and jackets on the bed. When he heard people leaving, he got up to say goodbye, but only with an effort.

In his sophomore year, Warren took an introductory course in Psychology and there discovered that his problem was not unique, as he'd thought, but part of a much larger Western crisis known as Identity and Authenticity. His textbook had a whole chapter dealing with just those problems. He was delighted to find that he was part of an endless tide of people who did not know who they were. In his inauthenticity and lack of identity, he was yoked irrevocably to mankind. He began to read Kierkegaard and to keep a journal. He also brought up existential subjects in conversations with his new, more intellectual friends, all of whom had strong views which they expressed while smoking pipes. For several months the discussions quelled his anxiety and filled the void around him, but one night, after talking to his mother and father on the phone and hearing their tones of amused condescension as he described his new interests and friends, he realized that nothing had changed. If he were to return to his boyhood home and stand in front of the mirror in his bedroom, he would still see no one. The old dispensation was too powerful to be broken by a few books and a few late-night bull sessions.

Later that year, Warren found himself reading Boccaccio for the first time. Although in this edition the sexy parts were in French, he could usually figure them out. The erotic images would pour through him for days afterward—the lustful hermits and lascivious nuns, the obliging servant girls and gardeners. One night he propped the book next to his typewriter and copied out the sexy parts in English translation. Then he lay in bed and read them while playing with himself, hoping that his roommates couldn't hear the juicy squeezing noises. He had always enjoyed playing with himself but tonight, due to the Italian's gift of erotic invention, he found the sensation particularly exquisite. And then, just as he was imagining that he was the novice in the nunnery and the handsome young gardener was mounting him among the hoes and rakes, his penis gave a jerk and spat out a milky liquid. He jumped up and went to the bathroom and washed thoroughly. For the next few days he was upset and puzzled, but a chance remark by a friend about wet dreams cleared it all up. The liquid on his tummy was the same stuff that had stained his bed while he slept. This had first happened when he was thirteen and his mother, discovering it, had changed the sheets without comment. Something in her elaborately nonchalant manner told him not to ask questions and thereafter, whenever it happened, he would say casually, "I think you'd better change the sheets." Now, the discovery that his nocturnal pollutions and the jack-off liquid were one and the same came with the force of revelation. He was seventeen years old.

In the following weeks he began to wonder if all the men in his class jacked off at night. It didn't take him long to realize that they did and, in a rush of joy, he decided that this habit connected them all in a profound and vital way. Of course, they probably didn't used typed translations of the *Decameron* to get going, but that was a minor detail. The end result was the same. Now he was truly in the majority.

However, when he thought about the matter some more, over the ensuing weeks and months, it came to him that his classmates were more likely to identify with the gardener than with the nun, as he had done. He had always known that he was secretly attracted to his own sex, but the fantasy in the convent garden brought it home to him more forcibly. He decided he'd better date girls more frequently, if he was to avoid the sense of isolation that the viciousness of his fantasies engendered.

Warren now made it a point to ask a girl to every dance held at school. The girls, who came from a nearby women's college, seemed delighted to be asked, and always loved the corsage he brought with him. But as the evening progressed, their animation would usually wear off and he would catch them looking longingly at other couples on the floor. These couples were either showing off with fancy shakes and hustles or were twined together like snakes. He himself preferred to keep a certain space between his partner and himself, although during certain slow numbers he felt obliged to press closer. Even then, by some discreet angling, he could keep his genitals out of contact. As they danced like this, he would think about Boccaccio, and the wild couplings between nuns and gardeners, and wonder how they ever got started. After each dance he would walk his date home and kiss her on her dorm steps, then walk home under the stars, relieved to find himself alone.

After a year of this he decided that the dances made him feel worse rather than better, and he stopped going altogether. On Saturday nights during his junior year he would go to the library or to a movie. He was aware that his old problem was ready to pounce and destroy, but somehow he managed to keep it at bay. Not long after this he tore up his *Decameron* translations—which were now dog-eared and dirty—and typed up some fresh stories of his own invention, starring the bodybuilders he had seen in *Strength and Health*. He would lie in bed as usual, reading the stories and playing with himself, but now he wore a jockstrap. This seemed to go with the stories, which tended to take place in locker rooms. In time his jockstrap became quite lemony with semen, but he could never bring himself to throw it away. Like a map of Oz, it bore the marks of rich and imaginary voyages.

It was during his senior year that he went to his first queer bar. Called the Chess Room, it was in the basement of a large hotel in Boston. Strangely, none of the guests in the hotel ever blundered in. Warren decided that the bellboys probably warned them away.

For three or four visits, Warren didn't speak to anyone. He just stood around, observing the protocol of approach and rejection, his hands sweaty around a warming beer. But at last he met his first sex partner who did not live in his imagination.

This was a man named Rudy, who seemed quite elderly to Warren, though he was only thirty. Rudy pressed his leg against Warren's as they sat at the bar, and followed this up with an embarrassed leer. At first Warren pulled his leg away, but after examining Rudy's sinewy throat and powerful hands, he let his leg drift back. This made his heart beat very fast and his hands sweat even more than usual. As Rudy talked, Warren managed to reply, wiping his palms on his pants from time to time. Half an hour later, knowing that nothing would ever be the same, he followed Rudy out of the bar.

Rudy lived in a basement apartment, which had a submerged and aqueous atmosphere, confirmed by the presence of water pipes overhead and a large tank of iridescent tropical fish. The place seemed fiercely remote from Warren's college campus, with its spacious quadrangles and ancient elms, but he thought that the submerged and murky atmosphere was probably a prerequisite to the subterranean act in which they were about to engage. Certainly standing in the center of the room with Rudy's body pressed to his was not something that could possibly happen in his dormitory. And letting Rudy kiss him was not even thinkable in his bedroom, with its rows of Modern Library editions and walls hung with football pennants. But here, in this dingy room below the level of the pavement, where disembodied ankles could be seen walking outside, such acts seemed natural, indeed inevitable.

After they undressed and lay on Rudy's studio couch, Rudy smiled and pressed Warren's head toward his groin, which was a tangled brush of dense black hair. But Warren was unable to perform the service Rudy wanted—it was too embarrassing and unfamiliar. Seeing this, Rudy laughed and swapped positions, and applied himself to Warren's cock with a cunning tongue. Warren had never seen his legs in this peculiar position—resting on the shoulders of an elderly man—and he had the impression that they didn't really belong to him. But this impression was soon lost in a sensation of intense pleasure and before he could stop himself he had ejaculated into Rudy's mouth. He thought Rudy would be furious, but instead he laughed again and lay down alongside Warren, cuddling him in his hairy arms.

They talked. Rudy asked him about college and he asked Rudy about his own life. He got the impression that it was a difficult and lonely affair. There seemed to be dangers everywhere—at work, in the bars, at home. Rudy sighed a lot and talked about not letting people know. With mounting sorrow, Warren saw that this was probably the future that waited for him. It was the logical culmination of the lewd stories he had been typing for so many years. His future would consist of furnished rooms, bar pickups and tropical fish. There would be something submerged and watery about it all. At the same time he had an acute sense of homecoming, as if this destiny had been arranged for him a long time ago and he was only now intersecting with it. Lying there, Rudy's coarse chest-hair scratching his own smooth chest, he understood that he had finally made a dent in his old problem. His reality was the same as Rudy's, the same as that of all the men like Rudy. For a moment, he fought against this notion, likening Rudy's room to Plato's cave, where only shadows danced on the wall and reality shone somewhere else, behind the shadows, still attainable, still embraceable—but he knew that this was just a literary conceit. Rudy, the other men in the bar, the love-making just concluded—these weren't shadows. They were as real as the dark furniture, the iridescent fish and Rudy's cunning tongue.

His life at college changed after that. He disengaged himself from dormitory life. It no longer seemed important or interesting. He found a solitary room, high under the eaves, where he could live without roommates. He spent most of his spare time in the library or going to the Chess Room.

He began to have sexual adventures of varied kinds—with military men, with traveling salesmen, with married men from Revere and Scituate. He became quite skilled at starting casual conversations and steering them to the desired outcome. He learned which hotels rented rooms to guests without luggage, and which movie houses had the darkest balconies. He was becoming, he knew, a sexual adept, and at times he felt quite soiled. But the notion that these encounters were advancing and defining his reality, helping him in his ancient quest, kept him from changing his ways. Sooner or later, he believed, these dark couplings with nameless men would crack the still-undeciphered code of his self.

But as his last year at college wore on, he found himself wondering more and more if this was going to happen. As his sexual encounters multiplied to two or three a day, he found himself, paradoxically, losing the strong sense of place he had glimpsed in Rudy's subterranean apartment. He wondered if sex in such large quantities, giving himself so totally to the embrace of men he did not know, used up what should rightfully have been his own. Sometimes he would lie in the dark of a hotel bedroom, next to a sleeping stranger, and pound his fist on the pillow, vowing that he would find what he was looking for, pin it down, give it a name. But by the next day, when he found himself cruising the streets again, he had forgotten his vow in the panic of the moment.

As his senior year came to a close, Warren decided that he would go to New York after graduation. The decision came to him one evening in April when he sat in the student lounge and listened to someone play the first movement of a Beethoven sonata. As Warren heard the lunging octaves and burnished glissades, a sudden lightness went through him, and he saw that a rich, satisfying life was waiting in New York. He would change his habits, which were still childish and collegiate. He would have a job, a career.

He moved the day after his last exam, too excited and impatient to wait for commencement. As the train clicked over the rails to New York, he recalled his first trip north four years earlier. Much had changed since then. A moment later he had a sudden view of his boyhood bedroom, and the mirror near the bed, and with a rush of pain he realized that if he stood in front of it now, his college degree in hand, he would still have trouble discerning the outline of his face. His father was dead, he had graduated with honors, he had learned to handle himself in the most delicate situations—but the most important thing had not changed.

He was depressed all the way to New London but there, for some reason, his mood changed. Perhaps it was being halfway to New York, or the lunch in the dining car, where he had sat with two freshmen from his college and patronized them horribly. But by the time he returned to his seat he was convinced that his quest was not hopeless. Thousands of young men had learned the secret of life in the stone chasms of Manhattan. He would find the answer too.

A few weeks after arriving he got a job as a trainee copywriter at one of the big agencies. It turned out that he had an easy flair for writing ads and was soon given more responsibilities. Although none of his college courses had prepared him for fashioning lines like "So firm yet so gentle," which the people at Scott Tissue liked enormously, he accepted his job without anger. It all seemed irrelevant to his real mission in New York. That took place at night.

He decided to look for a partner, someone with whom he might share his life, as the young men and women in his office did, in increasing numbers. One day, in a department store, he stopped in front of a big double bed, and looked at it hungrily, trying to imagine what his life would be like if he shared it with someone else—each with a night-table of his own and plenty of reading matter.

Whenever he met a male couple, he asked them questions about their life together, eager to find out if they conversed in the morning, wore each other's clothes and fell asleep at the same moment. These couples, with their aura of twinship, struck him as terribly real. Their doubleness was the badge of their authenticity. He wondered if this nostalgia on his part was not due to the fact that he had been an only child, and had been forced to people his solitary afternoons with imaginary playmates, but then dismissed the idea. He was attracted to the idea of coupling because he had been made not for struggle, for strife, for solitude, but for love.

Although he met many men in bars, none of them seemed much interested in domesticity. When he brought the subject up, they became offhand and wary. "See you around," was usually their final offering after an assignation, and Warren would sometimes wonder bitterly where "around" was. He finally decided it was in the men's wear department at Bloomingdale's.

As the months in New York lengthened into a year, then two years, he gradually gave up the dream of finding a twin.

He began to think of New York as merely a larger and more variegated cage than the one he had inhabited at college. This realization brought on a series of depressions, which gradually solidified into one big one. When he had been depressed for two months he began to think about professional help.

Warren chose a Freudian who interviewed him and told him he would be depressed as long as his physical and emotional urges were directed toward men. This seemed reasonable to Warren, who was then twenty-five years old, and was surrounded by a world intent on marriage and kiddie-cars in the suburbs. The Freudian, whose name was Dr. Craig, asked him to come every day on his lunch hour and lie on a couch. This was inconvenient—Warren went back to the office rumpled and abstracted—but there was no help for it. If you were going to be analyzed you had to go every day. Dr. Craig was a short bald man who did not enjoy speaking. At least he did very little of it. Instead he sat in a wing chair at Warren's head and listened. Occasionally he would fall asleep and Warren would wake him up by pausing in his narratives. Alerted by the silence, Dr. Craig would shift slightly, then say, "What happened after that?" Warren would be irritated but would proceed. As his sessions went on for months, Warren wondered when the breakthrough would occur. Moments of transcendent insight had occurred for all his friends who were in analysis. But this didn't happen for Warren. Although he talked about his parents, his cousin Ronnie, and his chronic sense of not being real, very little changed. He wept at the hurts and vowed vengeance for the wrongs—but an hour after leaving the gloomy office, the intensity evaporated and he was back where he started. Dr. Craig assured him that this would change in time if he continued talking and paying his monthly bills, which were enormous.

An additional prerequisite to success was to date girls. They talked about this a great deal. At last, despite his bad experiences at college dances, Warren invited a young woman to the opera. Mary Hallowell lived in his apartment house and liked to drink and sing—she gulped Manhattans during the measure rests in arias of the Italian baroque—and accepted with pleasure. After the opera, she invited him inside her apartment, but he made an excuse about the lateness of the hour and simply kissed her at the door. Her mouth was slack and her teeth protruded slightly, so that he had the impression he was kissing the porcelain enamel of a washbowl, but he moaned as if with sexual arousal and pretended to break away reluctantly. He never asked her out again.

As the years went by, Warren cut back on his sex life. Dr. Craig had made him feel guilty about his promiscuity. And the thought of a partner or twin was even less acceptable—it meant acceding to his urges in a way that Dr. Craig said was counterproductive. As for his old problem, Warren had learned a whole new set of terms for it. Identity and authenticity and nonbeing had given way to ego weakness, poor transference and lack of a suitable role-model. He sprinkled his conversation with these terms, usually among his friends who were also analysands, and was reassured by their approval. In the meantime he wrote prize-winning ad campaigns, tried with moderate success to stay away from a turkish bath for men, and masturbated a lot, forcing himself to describe his fantasies to Dr. Craig in technicolored detail.

Warren had refused to think about a future other than the one limned by Dr. Craig for so long—five years—that he was surprised one night, in a Village bar, to meet a man who made him think about marriage beds again. At this time he was thirty years old. The stranger was about his own age, of medium height, with chestnut hair and a granitic profile. His name was Gerald DeVane, and he was half-drunk. As soon as he saw Warren enter the bar, he came over, grinned in a lopsided way and began to rub Warren's belly through his flannel shirt. "I'm real good at rubbing bellies," he said.

At first Warren was annoyed and embarrassed but gradually he relaxed. He knew that this stranger would never write silly copy in an ad agency, would never pay an analyst half his salary for five years, and probably called his mother only once a year. All these qualities, strangely, increased the stranger's appeal, in a way that was quite the reverse of what he usually felt. Suddenly he decided that he wanted to spend the night with this man, who had now stopped rubbing his belly and was trying to hug him.

Gerald's apartment was a seedy sublet on the lower East Side. He had tacked some Monterey views to the bedroom wall. The bed, a mattress on the floor, was unmade. Normally this would have bothered Warren, but tonight it didn't. He had sensed something in Gerald that he had not encountered in years, if ever. He wasn't sure yet what it was but he decided to keep an open mind about the seedy apartment and the unmade bed.

After unscrewing the dangling light bulb over the bed, Gerald flopped down beside him. In the reflected street light, Warren could see that Gerald's skin was a silk coverlet, his muscles long and stringy, his spine a string of pearls. He could not seem to get enough of Gerald, through his lips, his eyes, his fingers. None of this seemed to have anything to do with the events of the past five years. In fact, as their lovemaking intensified, he had the impression that the self who had lived through those years had now been replaced by someone else, someone who had been curled up at his center like enriched uranium in a nuclear reactor, and was now permitted to stand free.

The next morning he found that his instincts had not betrayed him. Gerald was a nester. He didn't like solitude. When they journeyed together to Warren's apartment on the West Side, after a breakfast of eggs and cornbread, Gerald made himself instantly at home. In fact, he didn't leave for three days, going to his job as a temporary typist each morning and returning directly to Warren's apartment at night. He didn't worry about his mail or about the fact that he had left the lights on in his apartment. Gerald's homing instincts gave Warren some moments of alarm, as he realized his privacy was being encroached on. But he fought back his fears, understanding that if he was afraid now he would be afraid for the rest of his life, and that the enriched person at his core would never again stand free.

At his next session with Dr. Craig, Warren told him about Gerald. He talked about him for the whole hour. Dr. Craig remained silent until Warren began to discuss their plans for living together. At one point, momentarily apprehensive, he asked, "Do you think I'm doing the right thing?" There was a silence from the dark space behind his head and then Dr. Craig replied in his gloomy voice, "What does your conscience tell you to do?" Hearing this, Warren realized that his analyst had failed to understand what he'd been talking about. To him, Gerald was only another trick, another setback in the march toward heterosexuality. This struck Warren as not only insensitive but unfair and he began to tremble with anger. He had followed Dr. Craig's advice for five years and now that he had finally found what he was looking for, his discovery was being denied. "Conscience?" he heard himself say in a furious voice. *"Conscience?"* He swung up from the couch and looked directly at the small bald man in the wing chair who refused to meet his gaze. "My conscience tells me I should walk out of here and never come back." Warren was shouting now, his mouth stale with fear. He stood up, glaring at Dr. Craig, who seemed to shrink into his wing chair, his bald head glowing like the egg of some extinct bird. It occurred to Warren, looking down at Dr. Craig, that his connection with Gerald, despite being only a few days old, was deeper and truer than his connection with his analyst. It went back to his first reading of *Pinocchio* and to the mirror he had looked into so desperately while he was growing up. It went back to his disastrous boxing lessons and to his drinking bouts in high school and to his translations of Boccaccio. He also saw quite clearly that this was his story, not Dr. Craig's, and it was up to him to write the ending. If he did not write the ending now, it might never be written— it would remain open, and icy winds would blow through it until they rendered him as useless and empty as a house without doors or windows. And then he understood that he had always been real, always known who he was, but that he had allowed others, starting with his father, to tell him he was wrong. It had taken him thirty years to find out that there had been someone in the mirror all along, someone whom he had been denied the power to see.

"Goodbye," he said to Dr. Craig, who sat silently, looking sideways. "Goodbye," he said again as he closed the door. "Goodbye," he said to himself as he rode the elevator down to the lobby.

That night, after dinner, he took down his old copy of *Pinocchio,* now frayed and with a broken spine, and read the last chapter to Gerald, who had fixed hushpuppies for dinner and was wearing one of Warren's flannel shirts. When he came to the part where Pinocchio becomes a real boy, Warren put down the book and took Gerald's hand. Then he burst into tears. Later, after explaining how his long quest had started and how it had ended, he tore the ancient volume in half and dropped the pieces in the garbage. He never referred to it again, nor even thought about it, not in all the years he lived with Gerald DeVane or with those who came after him.

BORN IN MANHATTAN, Richard Hall grew up in the suburban town of New Rochelle, N.Y. After graduating from Harvard, he returned to New York City and, with the exception of three years in Puerto Rico, has made it his home since 1950. He has worked as a copywriter, music critic, teacher, film producer, editor and publisher. He is the author of the mystery novel *The Butterscotch Prince* (Pyramid, 1975) and several plays. At present he is contributing editor (books) for the *Advocate,* and is a member of the National Book Critics Circle. His articles and reviews have appeared in such diverse publications as the *New York Times, Village Voice, New Republic* and *Gay Sunshine.*

OTHER GREY FOX BOOKS

Daniel Curzon	*Human Warmth & Other Stories*
Allen Ginsberg	*Composed on the Tongue*
	Gates of Wrath
	Gay Sunshine Interview (with Allen Young)
Howard Griffin	*Conversations with W. H. Auden*
Frank O'Hara	*Early Writing*
	Poems Retrieved
	Standing Still and Walking in New York
Michael Rumaker	*A Day and a Night at the Baths*
	My First Satyrnalia
Allen Young	*Gays Under the Cuban Revolution*